"Charlie's a man!

"You know who's not a man? . . . none of us . . . to Charlie's people . . . We're animals. Aliens. We're alien animals come out of someplace else where we had a right to be, to here where we got no right. And you know what we do, now we're here? . . . we go and kill men and women—real men and women with a right here, because it's their world—in order to skin them and sell their hides to be shipped off the planet to other animals like us who don't even know where those hides came from.

"But Charlie, he's even more . . . Charlie can see an alien like me hidden in a dirty chunk of stone and carve that stone until it's art—until that alien's there for all to see.

"You and I can't do that; but he can."

But to some people, the Other is always alien, and alien art is no art at all; it's a threat.

ALIEN ART

by

GORDON R. DICKSON

ace books
A Division of Charter Communications Inc.
A GROSSET & DUNLAP COMPANY
360 Park Avenue South
New York, New York 10010

ALIEN ART

Copyright © 1973 by Gordon R. Dickson

An ACE Book

Cover art by David Plourde

First Ace printing: April, 1978

Printed in U.S.A.

To my mother, Maude Dickson

1.

The annunciator on the hotel room door chimed.

"Who's there?" asked Lige.

There was no answer. Lige did not move. He had been buying native art too long on these backward, newly settled worlds to open his hotel room door without knowing who wanted in. Also, he was pushing eighty now; and he was willing to miss an occasional deal rather than take risks.

"Who's there?" he repeated. "Speak into the annunciator —the black circle on the door."

"Mister," said a voice from the door, "I'm Cary Longan. I wrote you about some carvings a friend of mind did. . . ."

It was the right name. Lige put a twenty-second hold on the hotel security button by his phone and pressed it down. In twenty seconds he could find out enough to decide whether to flick it back up or let it sound.

"Open," he told the door. It slid aside and let in a typical New Worlds backwoodsman. The dress varied, as usual from planet to planet, but the smell was always similar. Wood-smoke, sweat, assorted native odors. This woodie was young, young and stringy.

"Mister, I'm Cary Longan," the woodie said, as the door

slid shut behind him. "I was to remind you your full name was Lige Bros Waters, you said in the letter."

Lige reached out and flicked the security button off hold. "Come on in," he said. "Have a seat."

Cary Longan looked uneasily about the hotel room. It was a room that had cost Lige less than half an interworld unit a day. Its carpeting was woven of native fibers, the walls were coated with a single color, and there was no such thing as a float chair in sight. The furniture sat heavily on thick legs, and was built of wood and fabric.

But the woodsman glanced about as if in a palace. He had recently shaved and carefully washed. But under the bony jawline, his thin neck was shadowed with uncleansed grime. In his leather and woolen clothes he looked half-starved and feral, a smoke- and dirt-stained whipcord of a man imprisoned by unfamiliar barriers to land and sky. In his hands he carried a homemade wooden box about ten inches on a side.

"That's all right," Lige said. "Come on, sit down. I pay for the room—people who come to see me can do anything I invite them to, here."

Cary came forward. He perched on the seat edge of a heavy, fabric armchair facing the bed on which Lige was sitting and passed the box into Lige's hands. Its weight was surprising. Lige almost dropped it. "They're in there," Cary said.

"The carvings your friend made?" Lige fumbled with the box, discovered that the top slid aside, and opened it. Within were a number of reddish-brown rocks, very heavy for their size. Lige took them out one by one and lined them up—there were six of them—on the bedspread.

He picked them up and turned them over, examining each again. He looked at Cary.

2.

"What is this? A joke?" he said.

Cary was leaning forward from the waist, painfully tense in his waiting. But when Lige spoke, the tension dissolved in puzzlement.

"Mister?"

"These—" Lige jabbed a forefinger toward them. "These are carvings?"

"Sure, mister," said Cary. "The ones I wrote you about. Charlie made them."

"He did?" Lige stared hard at Cary, but Cary still looked only puzzled. "Did you see him carve them?"

"Some," said Cary. "Some he did when I wasn't there."

"Carvings of what?"

"Of . . . ?"

"When you carve something," Lige said, patiently, "you make a shape like something you're looking at, something you know. These carvings are made to look like certain particular things, aren't they?"

"Things? Oh, sure, mister." Cary lit up. He reached out and easily picked up the closest of the rocks, holding it lightly between thumb and middle finger. Lige had needed to cup it in his hand to lift it comfortably. "See, this here's a fool hen sitting on its nesting hole."

"And this. . . ." He put down the first rock and picked up the one next to it. "That's a bitch swamp rat ready to have little ones . . . and this's a poison thorn bush mudded up for winter. This is a—well, it's a sort of a house Charlie lives in, himself. . . ."

He went on through the row, identifying each one. Lige stared at him a moment, then picked up the rock Cary had put down last and turned it over in his hands, looking at it from all angles. Cary waited, patiently but tensely; but when Lige exchanged the rock in his hand for one of the others, Cary got up suddenly and paced softly over to the room's one window, to stand looking out.

Lige put down the last piece of rock he had picked up and glanced over at the back of this man who had brought it, and the others, to him. Cary still stood, looking out. Beyond him Lige could see, through the transparent glass, a view of the park across the street, where voting booths were being set up, and beyond, the downtown buildings in Arcadia's Capital City. In every direction were the walls and tops of eternally new-looking, poured-concrete structures with glass pane windows. Except for the primitive nonvideo windows, it looked hardly different than any city on any other planet, except for those on the oldest and richest worlds. Bright scrolls of advertising signs filled the spaces among and above the buildings with color.

A HAPPY NEW MORTGAGE TO ARCADIA—THE FUTURE IN ONE GRAND STEP: EHEU AND KILLEY, CONTRACTORS/BANKERS, said one of the signs. JOIN THE RANKS OF INDUSTRIAL WORLDS: VOTE TO REMORTGAGE ARCADIA, cried another. TRADE THE WILDERNESS FOR PARKING LOTS, shouted a third.

Lige sighed inwardly. The promise of the signs was no less than would be delivered—although few of the native Arcadians would realize the full meaning of that delivery. All these new colonial worlds were alike—ready to sell their souls to industrialize in the hopes that they would become like Earth itself, or Alpha Centauri Four. Actually, the best they would ever achieve would be a cheap imitation of the richness of those older planets with their unbeatable head start. And the price would be deadly. If the man by the window could manage to stay alive until he was the age of Lige, he would live to see this Arcadia of his with the greater part of its natural resources plundered or de-

4.

stroyed, its atmosphere polluted, its native vegetation and wildlife killed off—all as the price of becoming, at best, a third-class industrial world.

For a moment the finger of temptation touched Lige. He was getting old, and he had never made that lucky find, that rare discovery those in his line of work always dreamed of stumbling upon, someday. It might be there was some truth to what the woodie said. It might be that the million-in-one chance was fact; that somewhere up-country, and soon to be lost forever on a world determined to go industrial, was a talent such as the field of art had not seen before—a talent that could make its own name, and Lige's as well, if Lige could discover it. But to hope for it was a foolish gamble. . . . Lige made up his mind. He spoke.

"Mister Longan."

Cary turned swiftly.

"Mister. . . ." His voice slowed at the expression on the other man's face. "Something not right?"

"I'm sorry," Lige said. "I can't buy these things."

Cary stared.

"But they're carvings," he said, "and you buy carvings, mister! The ad said so. Your letter said so—your letter I got right here. . . ."

He began to fumble inside his leather jacket.

"Sorry, no," said Lige. "Never mind the letter. I know what I said. But I don't just buy anything that's been carved. I buy art. Do you understand?"

Cary stopped searching under his jacket and let his hand fall helplessly to his side.

"Art. . . ." he echoed.

"That's right. And these aren't art," Lige said. "I'm

sorry. But if anyone told you they were, he was playing a trick on you, or your friend—what's his name? Charlie. . . ."

"Charlie. Well, that's what I call him. But, mister—"

"There's no art here," said Lige, firmly. "I buy art pieces to sell them to other people. Other people wouldn't buy these . . . pieces of yours and Charlie's. Maybe you can see them as representations of something; but I can't and my buyers wouldn't. They'd see them just as rocks—rocks that had been carved, maybe, but not into anything recognizable."

"Mister, I told you what they were—each one."

"I'm sorry. Maybe it's because I don't know the originals they were carved to look like—the fool hen, or whatever," said Lige. "But neither would the people who buy from me. Try to understand, Mister Longan. For me to buy it, your friend would have to make a carving of something I could recognize as a carving."

Cary's face lit.

"Like a man?" he said. "How about a carving like a man?"

"Yes," said Lige. "That's a very good example. Now, if Charlie had carved something in the shape of a man—"

"He did! He carved me, mister, long gun and all. Full size. It even looks like me. You'll buy that?"

Lige sighed, aloud this time.

"Well," he said. "I'll look at it. Bring it in."

Cary looked anxious.

"Can't hardly do that. It's pretty heavy, being full size. Maybe you'd come look at it. It's just a couple hours' fly inland."

Lige shook his head with a touch of relief.

6.

"I'm sorry," he said. He got to his feet and started putting the stones back into their box. "I'm leaving this afternoon for a couple of stops on the other habitated world in this solar system of yours."

The look on the woodsman's face made him add, rashly:

"I'll be back in ten days to pick up handicraft on your Voting Day from the people coming in. If you could have it here then, I could look at it."

"How much?" The words trembled on Cary's lips. "What price might you pay for something like that?"

"Impossible to tell." Lige hefted the heavy box and passed it into Cary's uneager grasp. He spoke briskly. "It could be anything. Two cents, or two thousand interworld units. We buy outright or sell for you on consignment, expenses plus a forty percent commission. Now, I've got to get at my packing—"

"One thing, mister," said Cary, resisting the slight pressure with which Lige urged him and his box toward the door, "I had to borrow money for an outfit to bring these here carvings to you. I was counting on selling them to have money for . . . I mean, I got to pay back, and it takes money besides to hire an airboat to fly back in and fly out with that big carving. If you could lend me just a little cash. . . ."

"Sorry," said Lige. He spoke over Cary's shoulder to the hotel room door. "*Open*. Forgive me, Mister Longan. I really have to pack. I can't lend you anything. It's not my money; it's the money of the company backing me. I have to account for it. Now, if you don't mind. . . ."

Cary let himself be pushed out. The door closed in his face. Numbly he went down in the elevator and past the people in the street-level register area. It was not until he found himself on the sidewalk outside that his mind began to work again. He went down the street to look for a public phone booth.

When he found one, he searched in his pocket for a smudged list of numbers and dialed the first one.

"Harry?" he said, when the party answered. "Cary Longan here, Harry. Listen, I need an airboat to fly upcountry and back, just one day. Going to make two thousand big units, Harry. Only thing is—"

"Hold it. Wait a minute," said the voice at the other end. "Are you talking about credit? Because if you are, Longan, forget it. You get a boat for cash—that's it."

"But listen, Harry—"

The phone went dead as the connection was broken from the other end of the line.

Cary dialed the second number.

Fifteen minutes later, his wide shoulders bent with defeat, Cary abandoned the phone booth. Still carrying the box, he walked on, aimlessly. After a while it began to register on him that he was out of the hotel area and into a section of small shops carrying farm goods and equally small bars—in the back section of the City. He passed one bar as the door opened and a man in a neatly pressed, slightly stained, white suit lurched out.

Cary cat-stepped lightly aside to avoid being blundered into and went on. A few steps later, however, his pace slowed. He stopped and went back to the bar entrance. For a moment he hesitated there, shifting the box from one arm to the other. Then, he went in.

Within, it was dimly lit, dark after the day-bright street. There was a bar all down one side with a long row of dispensers behind it, lit from below. The rest of the room was full of tables: slick, darkly gleaming tables. Cary, who had hesitated a second just inside the door, breathed out a little in relief and went forward to find a gap between empty seats, halfway down the bar.

The bartender, a heavy man, came along the other side of the bar to meet him.

"You aren't too high-priced here, mister?" Cary asked.

"No, we're not too high-priced, cousin," said the bartender, sourly, looking at him. "You found what you're looking for, unless you want to buy some packages of booze and take them back out in the scrub."

"What I was hoping for—" Cary put the box carefully on the bar, "was a length of weed."

"No weed. We don't like the customers spitting green all over the floor in here. You got money?" The bartender's voice sharpened.

"Money? Sure, mister," said Cary. "I just felt like a chew, is all. Give me a double—your cheapest booze and a beer."

The bartender turned away to fill the order. When he brought the glass and shot glass back, he thumped them on the bar in front of Cary, who had been fingering cautiously through a pouch he held in one hand.

"Fifteen cents, interworld—that's two dollars, local. Right, mister?" He fished out a single bill and dropped it on the bar. "I give you a five."

"Script!" said the bartender disgustedly, looking at it. But he picked it up, turned to feed it into the slot below the dispenser from which he had drawn the booze, then turned back to slide three one-dollar script bills at Cary. Cary picked them up cautiously and tucked them away before tossing down the booze and beginning to nurse the beer.

"Mister. . . ." he began, but the bartender was already off down the bar serving another customer.

Cary drank, and ordered again. And drank and ordered some more. The jagged, painful edge of hurt inside him at not selling Charlie's small carvings began to be blunted. A warm fog seemed to fill the room.

"Again, mister," he said to the bartender.

As the other brought the drinks back, Cary patted the box before him on the bar. "You see this, mister? Guess what's in there. Carvings, that's what. Want to see one—"

"Forget it, cousin," said the bartender, taking the five Cary dropped on the bar before him. "You showed them to me twice already."

He turned and spoke down the bar. "Rocks. Carved, he says, by some damn animal—one of those swamp otters, upcountry. That's all I got to do, is look at rocks!" He turned away, shoved the bill into the slot below the dispenser, and started off down the bar.

The warm fog cleared, suddenly.

"Mister," said Cary. The bartender went on. "*Mister!*"

The second time he said it, his voice was loud enough to quiet the hum of other voices in the now clearly seen bar.

"What's the matter with you?" the bartender said, turning and coming back up the bar to him. "We don't like shouting in here—"

His voice broke off in a gasp. His heavy body was jerked suddenly, halfway across the bar by one thin, hard hand clutching his jacket. Another thin, hard hand materialized only inches before his face, holding a dark brown, six-inch thorn.

"My change," whispered Cary. "You were going to cheat me, mister."

"Don't—don't scratch me with that!" The bartender yammered slightly, his jaw unhinged by fear of the poison thorn. "I got your change. I just forgot, that's all—that's all."

His hand came forward and dropped three one-dollar script bills on the bar. Cary let him go, gathered in the bills with his free hand, and backed to the door. All at once he was alone, outside on the sidewalk.

He looked about him, surprised. Night had fallen while he had been inside; but the artificial lighting made the street as bright as ever. No one was in sight.

He pinned the thorn back under the collar on his jacket and let out his tightly held breath with a sigh, relaxing. With a surge, the amount he had drunk took hold of him again. The fog did not move back in; but the whole street and its facing buildings seemed to take a sudden wild sweep halfway around him, then steadied again.

"Yeaaaahooo!" he yelled suddenly, tossing the box in the air and catching it.

Clutching his box, he reeled off down the street into a blur of gleaming concrete and more brilliantly gleaming signs.

2.

A jar, as if he had been dropped from some small height onto a hard surface, jolted Cary back to life. For a moment he felt nothing; and then a wave of nausea and a splitting headache took possession of him. He struggled to open sticky eyelids and looked up to see what seemed to be two men and a young woman. They were standing over him in a building that seemed to be a warehouse piled with trail goods.

"All right, men. Thank you," the woman was saying, crisply, in a voice he knew. "It's a Prayer Day, so I can't tip you. But come back here tomorrow after four in the afternoon and I'll give you thirty percent off on anything you'd like from the stock you see around you."

One of the men grunted.

"Took," he said. "We should've known, Jass."

"I beg your pardon!" The female voice sharpened. "Orvalo Outfitters has been in business twenty-three years and I'm an honest, religious city woman. If I say you'll get thirty percent off, that means an actual thirty percent off. Go check the lowest price from the other outfitters on what you'd fancy, then come back here and tell me. I'll give you thirty percent off that. You're being paid in dollars, pards, for a penny-rate job. It didn't take you five minutes to carry him here for me!"

"What if we don't have the spare cash to buy—" one of the men began, grumblingly.

"Then sell the discount to someone that has!" she snapped. "Do I have to think for you as well as reward you? Any more objections?"

Muttering, the two went out.

"Mattie," muttered Cary, mostly to himself, "you know you're going to make money, even at thirty per—"

Panic suddenly hit him. He jerked himself up in a sitting position, for the second completely forgetting the nausea and the headache, and stared about.

"My box!"

Then he saw it, on the floor within arm's length. With a gasp of relief he gathered it in and hitched himself backwards, so that he could sit, half-reclining against a pile of knapsack frames. Pain and sickness returned. He closed his eyes against them.

"That's right!" said Mattie's voice. Painfully he opened his eyes to see her standing over him. "You were holding it there under a truck-loading dock where you'd passed out. And the carvings are still in it! I can guess what that means. You couldn't even wait to see that buyer before getting drunk."

"Mattie. . . ." He rolled his head in negation against the hard edges of the frames that supported it.

"Don't tell *me*!" she snapped.

He shook his head weakly again, staring up at her. She was a tall, dark-haired girl of about his own age, with brown eyes in a tight-lipped, severe but almost beautiful face. She seemed to waver like an out-of-focus image to Cary's bloodshot eyes, as she stood above him, in a plain

13.

and rather stiff white suit-dress, white gloves, and holding a book bound in silver cloth. *Sermons for the Day* read the title on the cover of the book, in fiery red letters that gave the illusion of flaming and flickering as he watched.

"Mattie, how can I tell you if you don't let me talk?"

"Just answer me one thing!" she said, fiercely. "You saw the art dealer? Yes? No?"

"Yes!" he said. "That's what I'm trying to tell you. . . ." The room swam about him suddenly, and the headache was like an ax blade between his eyes. "Mattie . . . I got to have a drink."

She snorted. "From me? Not likely!"

He managed to fight back the discomfort enough to speak.

"I saw him, I tell you. I stopped by here first, too. Go look in the delivery bin below the wall slot of your office. I slid my guns and gear in there to keep safe, early this morning."

She breathed through her nose at him.

"If you're lying again. . . ." She whirled about, and he heard her heels tapping away through the warehouse and up the three steps onto the glazed, different-sounding floor of the outer office. The heel sounds ceased. Then they began again, coming back toward him. She appeared back over him, carrying the not-inconsiderable weight of his backpack, rifle, and handgun, which she threw down beside him with a crash.

"All right!" she said. "So you came by here. And you saw him. Why've you still got the carvings, then? He wouldn't buy after all, was that it?"

"Mattie, listen . . . I need a drink real bad."

"You're not getting one from me," she said. "Even if I wanted to, it's a Prayer Day. I won't handle liquor on a

Prayer Day. You talk—or I'll call the marshal's office to have you kicked out of town."

"No, Mattie. Listen. . . ." Cary licked parched lips with a dried rag of a tongue. "He took them . . . on consignment. He didn't have any place to carry them. He's coming back in ten days to pick them up."

"On consignment!" she cried. "That means you won't get paid and I won't get my money for maybe two months!"

"Not that long, Mattie—"

"I don't care! Two months is too long!" Her face was furious. "I need that money *now,* Cary. The New Worlds mortgage is going to be voted on in ten days. In a month, the factories and projects this world will get from remortgaging itself will already be building—"

"If there's enough people who vote to renew the mortgage—" began Cary.

"There will be!" she flashed. "Do you think a few woodies like yourself can stop the march of progress?"

"Aw, Mattie."

"Don't aw-Mattie me! Do you think a world like Arcadia is finished up, just because it's paid back the original mortgage its colonists signed, just to get them here and give them the bare essentials of survival?"

"But it's *our* world now, Mattie," Cary protested.

"Our world! Our mudhole! Look around you—" She threw out an arm furiously, pointing here and there about the room. "Do you think this is civilization? Earth had this much of things back in the nineteenth century, when stars were just little things going twinkle, twinkle in the sky—"

She broke off, suddenly.

"Oh, what's the use of talking to you?" she said, wearily. "You *like* a wilderness world. Well, I don't. And I want my money. When the new mortgage goes through, the money from it will finance an industrial expansion on this world like no one here's ever imagined. And I'm going to buy shares in the new industries with every cent I can raise. By the time you get shot to death, or die of some fever out there in the muskeg swamps, I'll be well on my way to being rich, with a decent roof over my head, and some decent appliances to make life livable, and my own private aircar. It's the first real chance for me or anyone else on this world since it was first settled, ninety years ago—but you don't understand that."

"I understand, Mattie," he said.

"No, you don't!" she said. "You don't understand anything but booze and that crazy swamp otter—"

"He saved my life!"

"I know!" she blazed at him. "You've told me. He saved your life. He carves rocks. What's that got to do with me, and how I've worked and slaved and sweated and held a job days while I tried to run this place nights and keep the business going? I've scrimped and saved and cut corners, and worked two shifts to get that money I lent you to bring those carvings down here and sell them! That script you drank up last night was *my* script! And I want it back!"

Guiltily, he fumbled inside his jacket and came out with his money pouch. She snatched it out of his grasp before he could open it and tore it open herself. She held it upside down; only a few local coins fell out.

"Well, I'll take your gear and guns for part of it!" She kicked savagely at his property on the floor beside him. "And I'll get a judgment against you for the rest and have you bound out to the City labor force, with your wages coming to me. There'll be ditches you can dig and errands you can run, if nothing else—"

"Mattie, listen!" Desperately, he broke in on her. "You

didn't let me tell you. The statue—he'll pay cash for that!"

She stared down at him with his pouch still held out in the air upside down. A single, crumpled script dollar floated down from it, ignored.

"What statue?" she demanded.

"You know—the statue of me Charlie made," he said. "I told you about it."

"Statue of you. . . ." Memory suddenly lighted her face. "That's right. You said he carved you, standing and holding a gun. The art dealer wants *that*!"

"It's like a man, that's the thing," Cary said. "It's recognizable. He'll pay cash, all right. Interworld units. . . ." He delayed a second, drawing the suspense out. "Two thousand."

"Two thousand!" The arm holding his empty pouch fell limply to her side. "That's more than the stock here and all I've been able to save, put together. . . ."

Her face tightened. She turned fiercely on him.

"You're lying!" she said. "You're lying again. Two thousand interworld units for a piece of rock chewed by a swamp otter! No one'd pay that!"

"No, Mattie. Truth!" he said. "You can call the hotel and find the record of my coming in to see him. He's gone off-world by now. Left yesterday afternoon, but you can check with the hotel. He'll be back in ten days—they'll have a place saved for him then, likely. Ask them. How'd I know that unless I'm telling the truth? He told me just when he was coming back and where, so I could have the statue down here for him."

She glared at him for a moment; but he faced her unflinchingly.

"Come on!" she said.

She turned and stalked off toward the office section. He

scrambled painfully to his feet and lurched after her, feeling his head throb with each footfall.

He followed her into the outer office, which was unchanged from the way it had looked when her father had been alive. It was a wide room, divided front from back by a counter running across the room except for a swinging gate at one end. She passed through this gate and he followed her—into the area holding two desks, the suspension files, and the office equipment.

"That's why I decided to have a few drinks to celebrate," he said. "That's why—"

"Be quiet," she said, sitting down at one of the desks. She punched buttons on the desk phone for the number of Capital City's best hotel. In a moment she was speaking to the reservations and information computer there. After a moment she punched off the phone and swung about in her chair to face him.

"See?" he said. "It was the truth, all of it. Mattie, I just got to have a drink—"

"What about this two thousand, now?" she interrupted him. "You have to deliver the statue down here to get it?" Her mouth tightened. "I suppose you want me to outfit and supply you again, so you can go upcountry and bring it down?"

"Well, you see, that's the thing. I can't just go up and bring it down overland. Not enough time. Also, it's too heavy. That's the thing, now. I got to fly up and fly back out with it."

"Fly!" She was on her feet. "Rent an airboat both ways? With my money?"

"Don't yell," he said, feebly. "Please don't yell, Mattie. My head—"

"Who cares about your head? Outfit you again—that's

18.

bad enough. Fly in one way—that's unthinkable enough. But fly up and cargo-fly back—it'd take most of the ready cash I've got!"

"Two thousand," he said, softly.

"Two thousand—two thousand—" she mimicked. But her eyes, focused on the wall, had grown thoughtful. She spoke more to herself than to him. "Fly up. Maybe. But down. . . ."

Her eyes came sharply back to focus on him.

"What's it weigh, Cary?"

"The statue?" He frowned, thinking. "Never really figured its weight . . . four, five hundred kilos, maybe."

"Four, five hundred kilograms. . . ." she muttered to herself. "Thousand, eleven hundred pounds, local, at five dollars' script the pound-mile. No, no . . . it'd break me. But fly up . . . eleven hundred pounds."

She broke off suddenly and looked at him again.

"We'll fly up and bring it down overland," she said. "There's time and I can outfit us from the stock here, so that won't take cash. What'll we need?"

"Mattie!" He stared at her. "Not overland. It can't be done. You don't know!"

"I know one thing," she said grimly. "It's coming down here overland or not at all. That's all I'm gambling on top of what I've lent you already. Not a penny more—not even for two thousand units."

She took a step back toward the desk and reached out toward the phone buttons.

"Take it," she said. "Or I'm calling the marshal's office right now and the statue'll never get here. I mean it, Cary!"

He stared at her miserably, his head splitting, his stomach floating queasily, and his thoughts floundering like stock deer caught in the mud.

"I don't know, Mattie," he muttered. "Maybe a man could. . . ."

"It's settled, then," she said. "I'll help you."

He stared at her.

"You?"

"Why not? You'll need help. I've been upcountry before. You know that."

"But, Mattie, even if I can do it, it'll be a terrible—"

"I don't care." Her face was stiff. "I'm not letting you out of my sight, this time, until you've got that two thousand in your hand. —And that's another thing. I get half of it. Half of whatever you get, now or later. We'll sign a paper on it. You understand?"

Cary wobbled his head numbly.

"What can a man say, Mattie?"

"Nothing. Because I'm right, as always. All right, we'll draw up that paper right now and pick out equipment. What'll we need?"

"Need." He forced the mired machinery of his mind to work. "Well, axes, of course. Block and tackle. And rope, plenty of it and strong enough to lift the statue—"

"Wait!" Sharply, she broke in on him. "Don't say another word about it. I forgot. The papers and the equipment'll have to wait. It's Prayer Day."

Cary frowned.

"We're going to need every day we got in ten days," he said.

"Can't be helped. I can't do business on a Prayer Day. It's not right and I won't do it. We'll wait for tomorrow— one minute after midnight."

"If you say so. . . ." He let out a weary breath and leaned against one of the tall file cabinets. "Mattie, though —seeing we're going to be pards in this, how about just one drink for me? I need it bad. You don't have to give it to me with your own hands. Just tell me where you keep your trade booze—"

"I'll help no one to liquor on a Prayer Day." She hesitated, however, looking at him a little less harshly for the first time. "I'll make you some coffee. Come on."

He followed her through a door into the back office, which she had set up as living quarters, converting it into a large, one-room apartment, with a cooking unit in one corner. Next to it was the accountant's desk stacked high with file cards from the disbursement company in town for which she worked a five-day week, regular hours.

"Sit down," she said.

Cary collapsed gratefully into a wide-armed inflatable chair and let his aching head loll against the yielding backrest. He closed his eyes as she went over to the cooking unit. In a minute or two, the mouth-watering odor of real coffee from the variform bean ranches down tropics-way made him open his eyes again. He opened his eyes, feeling humble. She could just as well have been close about it and given him synthetic. By her own lights, in her own way, she was a good woman.

She brought him a good quarter-liter mug.

"Many thanks," he said sincerely, taking it. The good smell was overpowering from the cup. He put it to his lips and sipped at it. Over the rim of the cup he caught sight of her watching him with a strange and unusual expression on her face.

"Cary," she said, as he lowered his cup, "how old are you?"

"Twenty-one," he answered.

"I'm nineteen," she said. "You know, if we'd been born back on one of the rich old worlds, you and I both'd be still in school with years of learning to go yet before we were off on our own."

He laughed, the noiseless laugh of a woodsman.

"You might be in school," he said. "Not me." And he drank again, gratefully, from the coffee cup.

Her face tightened up again.

"Meanwhile," she said dryly, sitting down and picking up her silver book which she had laid aside to make the coffee, "as long as you're sitting there drinking my coffee, I might as well be reading my sermons. I'll read out loud so it'll be to your benefit too."

Hastily, he put the coffee cup down on a side table.

"Mattie," he said, starting to get up. "Come to think of it, maybe I ought—"

"To what?" she cut in. Her eyes were dangerous.

"Nothing. Nothing, Mattie. . . ." He sank back into the chair and picked up the coffee to sip at it again. "Mighty fine and nice, this real coffee."

"It ought to be, at what it costs." She opened her book. Cary leaned back as she lowered her head over the open pages, closing his eyes and filling his nostrils with the rich smell of the hot coffee, trying to fill his mind with being back in the upcountry.

"Sermon Eighty-three," read Mattie, in a clear, penetrating voice, "by Alman Michaels, on The Law of All Things Made Right. *'Never doubt that there is a law that governs all things in the universe. Never doubt that law governs you. Never doubt that by that law all things in the universe are sifted, including yourself; that by it the flower is separated from the weed, the industrious from the unindustrious; and by that law the grain is saved while the chaff is thrown aside.*

" *'Moreover, entertain no doubts in what direction that*

chaff is cast. *For Hell always reigneth—another universe of torment eternal, to which shall go all who falter, who founder, who fail or flee. They shall be delivered into that which is far worse than that from which they shrank, into unending punishment. . . .' "*

3.

The airboat droned its heavy way inland, its rotors chewing through the upper air. Stretched out on the piled gear and equipment they were taking with them, Cary dozed in catnaps, waking momentarily to a reflexive alertness, then sinking back into a doze again. His hangover had almost worn off.

They had lifted above the neatly ordered, morning-white concrete shapes of Capital City shortly after dawn, having gotten everything ready in the hours between midnight and five A.M. Almost immediately they were above the farm country to the east and north of the City with its black earth and dusky green variform oaks and maples. They had flown above these colors and the morning brightness of rivers winding down to the coast for nearly twenty minutes. Now the farmlands were giving way to patches of forest even more dusky than the trees of the farm belt, for here among the variform plants of Earth, the first few native varieties were to be seen.

Up front, seated next to the airboat driver, Mattie kept up a running, argumentative conversation. Snatches of this came to Cary's ears in his moments of wakefulness.

24.

". . . your prices are outrageous, anyway!" That was Mattie.

"What else?" That was the driver. "You use complex equipment, it costs. Shoes are cheap. Riding cattle not much more. Hovertruck starts to cost—not just turbine fuel. Parts and upkeep. Naturally, airboats need more parts, and we can only make those by hand in machine shops. . . ."

"Ten months after the new mortgage gets voted in, pard, your 'boats'll be made by automated machinery, at a dime a dozen."

"Sure. But by the time they're that cheap, I'll be driving plasma craft on intercontinental hops and you'll want to hire one of those for whatever, and it'll cost you ten times what this boat does."

"By that time," Mattie's voice was sharp, "I'll be making fifty times what I do now; and I'll be able to afford it. I'm buying into more than one private subsidiary factory. When production starts in the big government general factories built with the mortgage credit, the companies I've invested in will get the subcontracts. I plan to be rich."

"Better than factory shares, then," said the driver. "You ought to put your money in timber and water rights. That's what I'm going to do. There's millions of board feet of lumber just waiting to be mowed. Throw in a few big dams and you've got hydroelectric power and cleared land for highways and industry. Hell, there's going to be men getting rich from garbage dumps alone, upcountry, if they got the sense to stake them out in the right spots. But raw materials and power are the sure bets."

"Maybe for fifteen years from now," said Mattie. "But I want my money while I'm young enough to enjoy it. . . ."

Vaguely troubled by the talk—just why he could not say —Cary dozed off again.

When he opened his eyes the next time, the forest belt was past and they were above rolling foothills covered with a tweed-like coat of cattle grass in which stalks of green, dull red and dark, dead brown, were intermingled. Occasionally a clump of scraggly native bire trees, their twisted low, ungainly shapes with fur-like tufts of green along their naked-seeming black limbs, broke the grassland scene.

". . . everybody but the cousins," the pilot was saying up front. "The farm hicks and the woodies like your friend back there."

"Don't be so sure some of them won't be investing in the building from the new mortgage too," retorted Mattie's voice.

"Come on, Mattie! What've they got to invest? The farmers, something maybe. Upcountry, they've got nothing. They probably won't even come in to vote—and we almost won't need them if the farmers turn out. Farms and cities can put together sixty percent of the population. We only need two-thirds voting to remortgage."

"If we don't need them, why all the free food and booze signs going up for the day before voting?" demanded Mattie. Back with the gear, Cary's ears pricked up. He had not noticed those signs when he was in town—too occupied with the art dealer and drinking. But if they could get the statue in at all, no reason they couldn't get it in a day early. . . .

He dozed off again, dreaming of free food and drink.

A jolt of the airboat as it dropped suddenly in an air pocket brought him awake again. Up front, for once, there was silence. Mattie and the driver were taking a rest from

26.

their talking. Cary looked out the small window beside the pile of gear on which he rested.

Below them now was the low ridge-mountain country, ragged, sloping, and cut by swift-running shallow rivers. He put his face next to the window and tried to see ahead as far as he could. He caught sight of the dull brown wall of cliff rising sharply three thousand feet to the plateau area on which was the highland swamp where Charlie and his kind lived. Lucky, thought Cary fleetingly, it was high summer. Winter would make it easier on the plateau itself, skidding the statue out over the ice. But down the cliffs in winter, with ice-toothed winds cutting into them, and sudden blizzards of smothering snow. . . .

"You never did tell me what you're after, up there." The sound of the driver's voice broke into the silence and Cary's thoughts abruptly.

"That's our business!" said Mattie.

"Just wondering. Your friend could be going fur hunting on those swamp otters; but you aren't in that line of work."

"He's not a trapper."

"Looks like one."

"He was once. Now he's made friends with the swamp otters. He protects them."

"Protects them?" There was a little pause. "You're buying me one, Mattie."

"Believe what you want, pard."

"But what's the percentage in *protecting* them? You can sell hides, how can you sell pro—" The driver's voice changed tone suddenly. "There isn't some kind of gemstone deposit up there, these otters can get at?"

"If there was," Mattie's voice was tart, "you'd be flying us back."

There was another pause.

"Sure. I guess so. Can't figure that otter business, though. . . ."

Cary dozed off briefly and woke again as the airboat tilted to climb to the plateau altitude. Cary raised himself on one elbow and looked out.

Just ahead now, the nearly vertical cliffs rising to the plateau were like bastions of dark granite. Here and there upon them a poison thorn bush clung, its white summer flowers looking speckled by the near-invisible dark clumps of thorns surrounding them. Nothing else grew on the cliffs.

The airboat mounted on the updrafts along the cliff face, flying alongside the cliff and rising as it went. After some fifteen minutes, it lifted above the edge of the plateau and Cary saw once more the black and gray-green tableland of the swamp where Charlie's people lived, and the bare earth stretched beyond interspersed with poison thorn, snake trees, native cactus, and clumps of bire, temp, sourbark, and upland vine.

". . . where do you want me to set down?" the driver was asking. Mattie's head turned and her face looked back at Cary.

"Where, Cary?"

Cary got himself up from the pile of gear and crouched forward under the low roof of the airboat until he was able to look between the two heads there and ahead through the windshield.

"See that clump of bire, about ten o'clock over there?" Cary pointed. "The one with open water nearly all around it?"

"I got it," said the driver.

"Take a line on that, mister. About eight, maybe nine klicks straight on, you'll come over some dry ground, a sort of spit coming out from the land beyond. We'll be setting down about there. I'll tell you just exactly when we get there."

"Eight-plus kilometers. Right," said the driver, starting his short-run log from zero. He flew on. Cary watched the log as its numbers slowly mounted toward eight point zero. Just before it reached that number, he spoke again to the pilot.

"You see it up there now, mister? You can tell where the ground starts because of the swamp grass being darker there."

"Right," said the pilot again. "I see it."

"We'll want to set down where you see a sort of star-shaped earth patch. There's a log hutch there with a vine roof that's gone black from being out in the sun. That's mine. You go down there."

"Right."

The airboat slanted earthward. A few minutes later it came to rest in the clearing Cary had described. They started unloading.

"Sure you don't want to make a pick-up date?" the driver asked, before taking off.

"No," said Mattie. "We told you we wouldn't need you."

"Right. Shut the door. Luck," said the driver.

They shut the door and the airboat waddled forward some forty feet before becoming airborne. It droned off to the southwest, leaving them standing between the dark earth and the dark blue sky with its swiftly drifting white clouds. A cool wind blew about them, although the sun was warm.

"Real pretty country, isn't it?" Cary said.

Mattie glanced about her, at the flat landscape with its dingy swamp grass leaning this way and that in thick patterns under the varying pressures of the wind, its black water, and its few dark clumps of taller vegetation. Rustles, squeaks, and whistles sounded from the swamp, with an occasional deeper sound something between a boom and a pop. Seeing she was not going to answer, Cary walked over toward the swamp side of the clearing, put his hands on either side of his mouth, and gave a long, fluting whistle. He waited, then whistled again. Then once more.

No answer came back from the swamp. He turned and walked back to the center of the clearing.

"What's that?" Mattie looked sharply at him. "Are you calling this Charlie otter of yours?"

"Not calling. Just passing the word I'm here." Cary revolved slowly about, head up, sniffing the air. "Something off here. I need to ask Charlie about that."

"You can *talk* to him?"

"Some," he said briefly, almost curtly.

He turned abruptly on his heel and started off into the swamp grass.

"On second thought, I'll look about a bit," he said. "You set the gear up."

Before Mattie could argue, the tall grass closed around him. He walked easily through it, for it was nowhere so thick or matted here as it was where it grew directly out of the water. After a moment he emerged into open ground again, where a little strip of swamp shoreline showed.

He crossed the clearing, closely examining the dry, blackish earth of it as he passed, and went on into the grass on the far side, following the pattern of the shoreline. It was not until the fifth small clearing he encountered that he found something interesting—a stick-like piece of hard, half-round black earth about two inches long and half an inch thick. He picked it up, nodded to himself and, still holding it, returned to the clearing where he had left Mattie.

She had sorted their gear and slung one of the self-supporting hammocks—not inside the cabin, but outside, in the middle of the clearing.

"I looked in that hutch of yours," she greeted Cary. "It's a mess. I'm not going to clean it up for you, and I'm not going to sleep in it either. I slung my hammock out here. It'll just be for tonight. Tomorrow we'll start moving the statue to town."

He turned without answering her, walked over to the door of the hutch, and opened it. He looked inside.

"Sure," he said softly. He came back to the pile of gear, took his rifle and ammo belt, and thumbed a smoke cartridge into it. He held the rifle up in one hand casually and fired it skyward. The white plume of smoke mounted toward the clouds.

"What're you doing?" demanded Mattie.

"I'll give him until the morn," Cary said.

"Him? Who're you talking about?"

"The mister that messed up my hutch," Cary answered. He laid down the rifle and held out his other hand to her to show the piece of earth he had picked up. "Mud from a boot cleat. He's swamp-wise enough to take off his boots in the water and come ashore in mocs. But he hung his boots at his belt and some of the mud in one of the cleats dried and fell out."

"You mean there's another woodsman around here?" Mattie asked.

"Unless he's left already," said Cary. "I'll sling out here and ask him to clean up in there for me tomorrow."

"Where's the statue?" asked Mattie. "I want to see it."

He looked at her.

31.

"Close," he said. "Put your boots on. It's wet all the way."

She complied, pulling on the heavy wading overboots and rolling their elastic tops up her legs as high as they would go. Cary led her off into the swamp. After a twenty-minute slog through the ankle- to thigh-deep water and the matted marsh grass—not so tall, here in the water, but much more thickly grown together—they emerged onto something like a small island overgrown with the marsh grass.

"Why did this Charlie put it way out here?" demanded Mattie. She was panting. Cary looked at her. She was not used to the marsh boots. She had been trying to lift each foot directly from the sucking mud at each step, instead of breaking the heel loose first to cut down the suction.

"He didn't put it," said Cary, pushing through a stand of marsh grass ahead of her toward the crown of the island. "It came up here. Swamp mud pushes rocks up every spring when it thaws. Most're not this big, though."

As he spoke, he broke through into a small clearing; and there, surrounded and hidden by the grass, was the statue.

It stood leaning at a slight angle above the black earth in which its lower end was still sunk. It was a narrow finger of a rock now—whatever its original shape had been—and as tall as Cary. Like the earth which had given it up, the statue was black—but it was a different color black than the soil. The black of the rock was like the black of Earth obsidian, in that when the sun caught its surface at a certain angle, the surface there looked gray. Somehow, standing as it did in the high-altitude sunlight, the marsh grass leaning to the wind behind and all around it, the statue seemed a natural part of its surroundings in spite of its carved shape.

Mattie stared at it.

"Not much of a statue," she said after a moment. "Hardly make out it's a man with a gun, let alone you. . . ." She hesitated, still staring at it. "No, there's something about it like you, after all. But I don't know what."

"You like it?" Cary asked.

She shivered slightly.

"I don't know," she said, in a lower voice. "It scares me, a little."

"Nothing to be scared about," said Cary.

"I don't mean scared, like . . . scared," she said. "I mean . . . it just makes me feel as if we shouldn't move it from here, maybe."

"We can move it any place we want," Cary said. "It's a statue of me, Mattie."

She pulled her eyes from the statue and looked about the ring of tall, surrounding swamp grass.

"How are we going to get it through the swamp?"

Cary smiled.

"You were the one so sure we could shift it down to the town," he said. "Don't you know?"

Mattie turned on him.

"I don't know the upcountry like you do!" she said. "Of course, I was counting on you to figure out how to move it!" She lowered her voice. "I suppose we'll have to build a raft or something and float it through the swamp to the edge of the plateau."

"No trees up here make logs that'll float," said Cary. "Also, too many spots too shallow for floating a raft through."

"All right," said Mattie. "You tell me, then. You must've had some idea when you said we might be able to bring it down overland."

Cary nodded.

"Sledge," he said.

"Sledge?" she echoed.

Cary nodded.

"Right," he said. "Couple of good, round-bottom runners with turned-up ski noses, slats across them. Dried grass mats on the slats to swell up around the statue and keep it from rolling off. The statue'll be under water most of the time—that takes half the load off. Smooth runners'll slide through the muck of the bottom nice and easy without getting suction-caught."

He turned abruptly.

"Better get back to the gear and at it. Take all afternoon to make."

They returned to the clearing where Cary's hutch sat. On the way in, Cary gathered a huge armful of the land-growing swamp grass; and once they were back he demonstrated to Mattie how to take fist-thick bunches of the long grass and plait these together to make mats.

". . . doesn't matter much if the mat holds together pretty loose for now," he wound up. "Once the stalks get wet and start swelling they'll hold together just as if they grew so. You go ahead. I'll go chop logs for the runners."

He took an ax and some rope and went off into the grass. Shortly, Mattie heard the sound of chopping, and in a little while he came back into the clearing, dragging two roped-together chewbark logs about ten feet long. As Mattie, plaiting the grass mats, watched, he went about making his runners.

He cut a deep V-shaped notch with the ax about a hand's length back from the end of one of the logs. Then, turning the log on its side, he split it in half from the notch back to the other end, leaving a length of half-log with a full thickness of head on it. Rapidly, using the ax, he barked this, exposing the smooth wood underneath. Then, turning the barked half-log upside down, he took the ax high on the handle near its head and proceeded to use it almost like a jackknife, to whittle the head-thickness into a curved angle.

When he turned this back over on its rounded underside, he had what was very plainly a runner with upcurving front end for the sledge he had described. Turning to the other log, he duplicated the procedure. Then he went into the hutch for a moment and returned with a long pair of obviously hand-split boards. He cut these into lengths and nailed them crosswise on the two runners.

"There she be," he said, putting the ax aside. He looked over at Mattie. "How're you coming with those mats?"

Mattie blinked and looked down at her hands.

"I've almost finished the second one," she said.

"We're going to need about eight," Cary said. "I better give you a hand." He looked up at the sun, which was now down close to the western surface of the plateau, the land beyond the swamp. "We'll be ending up by firelight as it is—"

He broke off suddenly and looked back toward the swamp.

"Mattie," he said. "Stay put where you are."

In three long, quiet strides he reached the pile of gear and picked up his rifle. Tucking it under one arm, barrel pointing down, he turned to face the stand of grass into which he had walked earlier to find the small piece of dried mud from a boot cleat. He stood balanced, legs a little spread, facing in that direction, but tense as some wild animal on the alert.

Mattie gazed at him startled, her hands gone still on the ropes of dried swamp grass. There was nothing visible to call forth such a reaction in him.

"Cary—" she began.

"Hush," he said.

She looked from him to the grass and saw nothing. Then, without a rustle, there was suddenly another woodsman standing just inside the clearing at the edge of the grass. He was a bigger man than Cary, heavy-bodied, with long legs and a short gun holstered at his hip. He carried his rifle in the crook of his elbow, barrel waist-high. For a moment he seemed so like Cary in dress and attitude that he looked related.

"Mister," he said to Cary.

"Afternoon, mister," Cary answered. "Drink and eat a bite?"

"Thanks kindly, no. I ate some already."

"Sad to hear it, mister," said Cary. "You saw my smoke?"

The other shook his head.

"Must have been looking otherways," he said.

"The airboat?" Cary said.

The other only looked at him.

"Well, I tell you something, mister," said Cary softly, after a moment. "These swamp otters here aren't for trapping."

The other woodsman gazed back and cradled his rifle a little more closely.

"Free country," he said.

Cary shook his head slightly.

"No, mister," he said. "Not this place."

"Cary—" It was Mattie suddenly speaking.

"Shut, Mattie," he said, without raising his voice but

36.

without taking his eyes off the other man. "You hear me, mister?"

The woodsman gazed at him for a long second without movement or change of expression.

"Mister," he said at last, "you must think you a real Cary Longan."

"Happens I am," said Cary. "That's me, mister."

The larger woodsman continued to gaze at him steadily, this time for several seconds.

"Heard you was placed elsewhere. If it's you, then——" he said at last.

"Heard wrong," said Cary. He did not move, only stood waiting.

Slowly, almost without his seeming to have anything intentional to do with it, the rifle in the other's hand slipped out of the crook of his elbow and on down until its butt rested on the ground and he held it by one hand at the muzzle end of the barrel.

"Guess I did, mister," he said. "I'll be moving on then."

"We'll be moving on likewise, in the morn," said Cary. "Makes no difference. I'll be back."

"Sure," said the other. "Makes no difference."

He looked for the first time from Cary to Mattie and nodded his head at her.

"I'll say you both good night," he said.

"Mister," said Cary.

The eyes of the other came back to him.

"My hutch back there," Cary said, jerking his head at it. "Might be you'd take a look at it sometime before you pack up and leave for good."

The other looked at the hutch and back at Cary.

"Sure. I'll do that, mister," he said.

Abruptly, he was gone. Cary walked back to the pile of gear without a word and laid the rifle back down. But he picked up his gunbelt with the short gun in it and strapped it around his narrow waist. Looking up from doing this, he caught the eyes of Mattie upon him.

"Sorry about saying you shut, Mattie," he said, mildly. "I didn't just have the time to talk with you then."

She looked at him a second or two longer, and then without a word went back to her mat-making. He came over, sat down cross-legged on the ground on the other side of the pile of pulled, dry grass stems, and began plaiting.

They worked industriously until the light began to dim. Then Cary built a fire while Mattie cooked supper on the wick-stove they had brought along. After supper, by the light of the fire, they took up the making of mats again. Sometime during the evening, with the darkness like a wall all around them, the stars overhead, and the fire burning warmly in front of them, she spoke, unexpectedly:

"When's that Charlie otter going to show up?"

"Don't know he will for sure," answered Cary, looking up at her from his plaiting. "Hope so, though."

"I'd like to see him," she said. After a moment she added, "You know what it is in that statue that makes it look like you? It's because it stands the way you stand, sometimes—like you stood when you were talking to that other woodsman today."

"Why, how'd that make it look like me?" he asked.

She glanced up and her eyes met his.

"Everyone stands a little different," she said. "Your way's like nobody else's, and I recognized it in the statue —that's all."

He nodded, a little wonderingly.

"I guess that's true," he said. "Everyone's different."

38.

They finished their mats and turned in. At first light of dawn they woke and made breakfast. They were just about to sit down with their plates when a sharp, prolonged whistle made them turn about.

Mattie took a sudden, reflexive step backwards.

Less than fifteen feet away, just out of the swamp water onto the shore, sat a sleekly black-furred creature about four feet long in the body and looking as if it weighed as much as a man. It had a long, sinuous neck and head that was otter-like in every way, except for the glint of long, flat, sharp-edged teeth between the black lips.

4.

"It's Charlie all right," said Cary. He whistled.

Charlie gave a chorus of whistles in return and came up the slope from the water to them, moving suddenly and very swiftly. He did not hump himself along like an Earth otter, but instead undulated up the slope on his short legs, with a snake-like motion. Still whistling, he stopped for a moment before Cary, pointed his head for a second at Mattie, then circled the sledge, moving his head over the items of gear already on it, as if checking each one of them out.

Cary whistled, and Charlie paused to lift his long neck to look at him. Cary patted himself on the chest, pointed out over the swamp, whistled again, and stepped over to squat down and pat the sledge. He was whistling steadily meanwhile—short sharp notes in several different tones. He moved his hand in a circle over the gear, stood up, and moved to the front of the sledge and pulled on one of the drag ropes attached to it, so that the sledge moved forward slightly. Then, dropping the rope, he went over to Mattie, put his arm around her shoulders, and rubbed his cheek against hers.

Mattie gasped and tried to pull away, but his arm held her immobile.

"Sorry, Mattie," Cary said, "act like you like it. This is the way they rub heads with each other."

"You shave from now on, if you're going to try something like that!" snapped Mattie—but her voice quavered on the last words.

He let her go.

"Sorry, like I say," he said. "I was just trying to explain to him about the sledge and all."

"And me—what was that supposed to mean? I suppose you told him I was your mate or some such thing!"

Cary smiled slightly.

"Well no, Mattie," he said. "I just told him you were female and left it at that. Don't go worrying about what he understands. He's bright enough, but I can't really talk to him much more than in sign language."

"You seemed to be doing all right," she said.

He shook his head.

"We're too much different, us and his people," Cary said. "He says he understands about the statue and the sledge, but I don't really guess he does. Anyway, he'll find out when we get to the island."

He turned back to the fire and squatted, picking up his plate.

"Come on," he said. "We better finish up here and get going."

They ate and finished loading the rest of their gear on the sledge. Then, with each one of them on a drag rope, they pulled the heavy sledge down into the swamp water. It followed tautly at the end of their lines and nosed down out of sight below the surface.

But as it touched the mud, the change in the effort required to drag it was immediate and startling. It glided at the end of the drag ropes, somewhere back there, a foot or so under the black face of the swamp water. Mattie could pull it easily alone. In fact, there was less effort to the pulling than there was to the walking itself.

"Remember what I told you," Cary said, sloshing alongside her and watching. "Break your heel loose first, then sort of lever your foot up, toe last, as you swing your weight forward on your other leg. Get the rhythm of it, sort of. It's like walking on snowshoes, only different. I mean, you got to get in the pattern of it."

Mattie tried, but it was still a struggle.

"I'll take the sledge to start with," Cary said, taking the rope from her. "You just concentrate on the walking."

"I can pull and walk too," said Mattie, grabbing for the rope but missing.

"Sure. And you'll get lots of chance to," said Cary, striding ahead effortlessly with the sledge following and Charlie swimming with just his nose out of water, smoothly alongside. Mattie floundered in their wake.

When they got to the island, Mattie took a rope determinedly, and this time Cary did not stop her. Together they pulled the sledge to the clearing where the statue waited.

Charlie had gone quickly on ahead of them. When they emerged into the clearing, he was up on his back legs, his front paws pressed against the stone shape of the statue, and his restless head searching over the stone surface before him. From time to time he whistled softly; and once his lips drew back, exposing the full four-inch lengths of yellow chisel teeth with which he made some small alteration in the shape on which he pressed those front paws.

Cary pulled the sledge up with one end against the lower part of the statue. It now seemed to lean threateningly above the gear piled on top of the grass mats covering the

42.

sled to a depth of at least a foot above the slats. He unloaded the gear, then dug down under the rear ends of the runners so that the back of the sledge settled and the back slat lay flat on the earth. Then he tied a rope around the upper part of the statue and ran it forward, around the front slat of the sledge and back, so that he stood beside the statue with the end of the rope in his hands.

"Mattie," he said, "stand on the front slat there. Help hold the sledge down." He whistled at Charlie; and as Mattie stepped up on the front slat, Charlie came with a bound to rest on the upcurving front end of one of the runners.

Cary took a couple of turns of the rope around his wrists and began to pull.

His heels dug deep into the dirt with his effort. For a moment it did not seem as if the statue was going to move at all. Then, slowly at first, then quickly, it toppled forward onto the sledge, sending out a spray of moisture from the newly dampened grass mats as it sank into them.

The statue lay embedded in the straw mats, almost hidden from sight among them, fairly in the center of the sledge. That part of it which had been underground, however, projected beyond the back of the sledge.

Cary rummaged among the gear and came up with what looked like a loop of thick wire between two small wooden handles. He unlooped the wire to give himself a length of perhaps two-thirds of a meter stretched between the handles, and with this began sawing off the extra rock at the statue's feet.

The abrasive wire cut smoothly through the rock. Charlie hopped off the sledge and ran back to sit, giving an occasional, almost whimpering whistle as he watched Cary work. When the end of rock finally fell off onto the ground,

43.

Charlie's head dipped over it and he examined the smoothly cut surface closely, before turning to examine the other cut face on the base of the statue.

Cary watched the swamp otter for a second as he recoiled the abrasive wire.

"Give me a hand getting this gear loaded back," he said to Mattie, turning away. Together, they got the gear back on and roped down.

"Take a drag rope now, if you'll be so kind," he said to her when this was done. Together, they leaned on their ropes. The sledge resisted for a moment, then moved grudgingly forward. They struggled with it at the limits of their strength until it entered the grass. With the crushed stalks under its runners, it moved a little more easily; and with the help of the slope, they got it down and into the swamp water, the top of the pile of gear barely showing through the surface of the water behind them.

"All right now, Mattie, stand clear," Cary said, "and I'll turn her."

Mattie let go of her drag rope and stood back. Cary moved in close to the invisible front of the sledge, took hold of both ropes, and tugged sideways, stepping back as the front of the sledge slued around.

Charlie, who had followed them from the clearing into the water, suddenly swam to the pile of gear on top of the sledge and climbed up on it. He extended his head toward Cary and gave a long, low, fluting whistle that was almost a wail.

Cary let go of the ropes.

"Now we have it," he said. He waded over to stand beside the sledge, looking at Charlie. Their heads were almost on a level and only a few inches apart.

44.

Cary whistled, and drew a circle with his hand, ending up with an outstretched arm pointing toward the edge of the plateau. Charlie went into a fluttering succession of small whistles in a large range of tones. Cary shrugged and, turning, went back to the front of the sledge and picked up a rope. Charlie whistled shrilly behind him.

Cary turned and whistled once. Charlie repeated the shrill whistle twice. Cary turned to Mattie.

"He's got it straight now," Cary said. "He says he's going with us."

Mattie stared.

"You aren't going to let him?"

"Rightly," said Cary, slowly, "I don't see how I could stop him."

"But he doesn't understand what he's getting into!"

"Sure doesn't," said Cary. "He thinks we're taking the statue to someplace where there's a lot of people like me who'll like it. It's the one big thing he did. He wants to be there to see them liking it."

"Can't you—" Mattie looked at the swamp otter. "Isn't there some way to explain to him it's not like that?"

"Tried," said Cary. "I told you his people and us are too different. How'm I going to explain money, and art buyers, and other worlds like this to him? I can't even make him understand what it's like off the plateau, properly."

"Then make him stay, for his own good."

Cary shook his head.

"Can't do that," he said. "Wouldn't be right."

"But can't you understand!" Mattie's voice was fierce. "He may not make it!"

"Likely, he won't," said Cary. His eyes met hers for a moment.

"Then you've got to stop him, don't you?" demanded Mattie. She watched him incredulously. "It's better for him to live, even if he doesn't understand why, isn't it?"

"Not surely," Cary said. He frowned, and stood thinking. About them the cool, high-altitude wind whistled faintly in the marsh grass and ruffled the surface of the dark water in which they stood. Charlie himself was motionless as a statue on top of the gear, seeming almost to float on the water. There were no clouds in the dark blue sky this day; and all about there were no light colors to be seen, only blue and black and brown and gray.

"If you're fond of him," said Mattie, in a lower voice, "you won't want him to kill himself for something he doesn't understand." He stood as if he had not heard her.

"No," he said, rousing himself at last. "But he's got a right, like anyone else. Come on."

He whistled at Charlie, who plunged off the top of the gear back into the water. Cary went back to take up a drag rope. Mattie picked up a rope herself and fell into step automatically beside him, looking up at his face. But her help was hardly needed. Even loaded, the sledge slid as easily through the bottom muck once it was started as if through a thick layer of grease.

Suddenly, the sled surged forward and their ropes went slack. Looking back, they saw Charlie's muzzle and a glint of yellow teeth at the edge of the sledge. He had taken some of the ropes binding down the gear firmly in his jaws and was swimming forward strongly, pushing the sledge as he went.

"Look out," said Mattie tartly, "or he'll run us down. Why don't you get four more of them to push and you and I could ride to the edge of the plateau?"

46.

Cary looked over at her and found her expression a good deal more gentle than her voice had indicated.

"The rest don't care for Charlie. Or me," he said.

"They don't?" she said.

"That's right."

"But you protect them from the trappers!"

"They don't believe I do so much," said Cary. "I've tried to tell them, but they don't believe me. They don't believe Charlie, either. See, they all make shapes with their gnawing on things. Their food's swamp clams; and their teeth keep on growing all their lives, so they've got to keep gnawing on things to keep them the proper length. But Charlie's the only one who got mixed up in making shapes with one of us people. They're kind of down on him because of it."

Mattie looked back at the powerfully swimming otter.

"You'd think they'd be proud," she said.

"Nothing to be proud of, way they see it," Cary said. "Any more than with us." He met her eyes for a moment. "Everybody human thinks I'm crazy to have doings with otters. The other otters think Charlie's crazy to have doings with me. Not much difference either way."

They splashed on through the swamp, stopping at noon on a small grass-covered island to eat.

"Will we make the edge of the plateau by dark?" Mattie asked.

"Ought to," said Cary. "Weather's good, and we've only got about another four-five klicks to go."

But after lunch they ran into a succession of shallow areas in the swamp that were too large to go around. It took all three of them, heaving together, to get the sled across a couple of long, dry islands that barred their path.

"Should be deep enough water from here on," said Cary,

47.

after they had crossed the second of these. He looked up at the sun, now nearly halfway down the western sector of the sky. "Still ought to make it by sundown."

They went on; and the wide, grass-tufted lagoons through which they had passed most of the day gradually gave way to what was almost a channel of thigh-deep water between walls of water-growing swamp grass some twenty meters apart. The close horizon of the plateau edge could already be seen, a reddish-brown ridge lifting above the tops of the grass and the water ahead.

They reached a point where the channel narrowed to less than twenty meters in width. As they passed through this neck of water, there was an abrupt chorus of shrill whistles, and swamp otters appeared from the grass on both sides of them.

Charlie, who had been pushing at the back of the sledge with Mattie pushing beside him, leaped suddenly up on top of the gear and whistled back at his own kind.

"Cary!" called Mattie.

There was a note of panic in her voice. Cary turned his head, still leaning against the drag rope on which he was pulling.

"It's all right, Mattie," he called back. "Don't figure they'll hurt us."

Mattie hastily abandoned the rear of the sledge and came splashing hurriedly up to join him.

"What is it? What're they here for?" she demanded.

"Charlie—and me," he answered, still slogging forward. "I told you they didn't think too much of him. Or me."

Mattie put her hands over her ears.

"I can't think!" she shouted to him above the whistling. "Look at them. Look at him!"

48.

From the grass on each side of the channel otters were making little dashes out at the sledge, then stopping and turning back into the stalks. Their long necks were outstretched and curved. Their lips were wrinkled back to expose their teeth, and they clashed them together, whistling and hissing at Charlie.

Charlie himself, on top of the gear, was transformed. His neck was also curved and outstretched; his lips were drawn back. He also gnashed his teeth, marching back and forth on the gear of the sledge as he did so, whistling and hissing first at the otters on his left, then at those on his right. As with some of the otters along the grass fronts, a yellowish form was beginning to cling to his teeth and lips. His eyes were bloodshot, and a sharp, acid-musky odor began to drift forward from him to Cary and Mattie on the following breeze.

Then suddenly, inexplicably, he stopped pacing and whistling and sat down on the gear. His jaws closed; his lips covered his teeth once more. He sat, staring back at the other otters, unmoving and silent.

Gradually, the whistling of the otters dwindled in numbers and volume. Their dashes at the sledge became less frequent and ceased. As the channel began to widen out, they gradually began to fall behind until the sledge was moving steadily away from them; and they sat silent in the water behind it.

Charlie lifted his head on its long neck and sent a long, fluting whistle back at them. They moved about in the water uneasily, but none of them answered.

After a while, Charlie repeated his whistle. Again there was movement among the dwindling figures behind him, but no answer.

Once more he signaled before the other otters were lost to sight in the glare of the westering sun on the water behind the sledge; and this last time as well no answer came back.

They trudged on toward the edge of the plateau. Then Charlie slipped off the gear and swam around behind the sledge to put his teeth in the ropes and push.

They moved on. The sun was just touching its lower edge to the western horizon of the plateau land when they tugged the sledge finally up onto dry earth again. It was not the black earth of the swamp but iron-rust-colored soil, studded with gravel and small boulders. Two hundred meters beyond them the ground disappeared where it sloped steeply away to the rock edge of the plateau cliffs.

"Start setting up camp, will you, Mattie?" Cary asked. "I'll go take a sight down the cliff while there's still some light to see by."

He went on across the two hundred meters of rock-strewn ground until his boots scuffed on bare rock, and he looked down at the steep slope leading to the cliff edge. Turning sideways, step by step, he went carefully down that slope in the dim light to where a wall of rock dropped off. He looked over.

It was hard to see in the gathering dusk, but the cliff proper fell away in a series of vertical drops to various shelves and pockets, in what amounted to perhaps a sixty-degree slope overall. His eye picked out a series of such shelves below him on which it would be possible to start lowering the statue. But less than fifty meters below him, all details were lost in the gathering darkness.

"Have to check it again tomorrow morn," he said to himself. "Don't want to get stuck on some ledge with no way out but back up."

50.

He returned to the shore of the swamp. Mattie already had most of the camp gear off the sledge and the wick-stove going. Cary himself built a fire; and as the new flames licked upwards, brightening their immediate vicinity but throwing the rest of the landscape into further darkness, he sat back, squatting on his heels, and looked over at Mattie.

She was moving about the business of cooking with automatic motions like a sleepwalker. He straightened to his feet and walked over to her, taking the spoon she held from her hand.

"My night with the grub," he said. "Lay yourself down a bit until supper's done."

He pushed her gently back to the pile of gear and made her sit there with her back supported by the unrolled sleeping bags. Then he went back to the wick-stove and the dried meat and rice she had already in one of the pots, covered with water, swelling and cooking. When he glanced over at her a few minutes later, he saw her still in a sitting position but deeply asleep.

He stirred the meat and rice mixture and looked across the fire to where Charlie lay, head upright on his long black neck, eyes fixed on Cary himself.

"So," said Cary. He whistled softly, and Charlie whistled back.

"All right then," said Cary. Quietly, so as not to wake Mattie, he began to sing across the fire to the swamp otter. Charlie responded with a series of accompanying low whistles and warbles that was almost like crooning.

The two of them were enclosed in the light of the fire, together, the otter with his head high upright and whistling, the man squatting on his heels by the low stove and singing. . . .

"Bonnie Charlie's noo awa'
Safely o'er the friendly main.
Mony a heart will break in twa,
Gin he n'er comes back again. . . ."

5.

The next day dawned with a gray overcast that extended solidly from one horizon to the other, torn only occasionally by the wind to show a ragged patch of the dark blue above. Sporadic bursts of sunlight from such rents found the camp from time to time.

As soon as the light was good enough to make out details, as far as the eye could ordinarily see in daylight, Cary was once more on top of the cliffs proper, sighting out a route downward from ledge to ledge toward the seamed and rugged country at the foot of the cliffs. This time Mattie and Charlie were with him.

"See there, Mattie," said Cary, pointing down the cliff face. "What we want is a route down with easy drops or slopes from ledge to ledge. Not more than eight-ten meters between ledges, for easy handling."

"Well, there's lots of that," said Mattie, gazing downward. "It doesn't look too hard."

"No, doesn't look hard," said Cary. "Harder'n it looks though—you'll see when we get down a ways. Also, there's two things to watch for. We don't want to get trapped with no ledge close enough below to reach, because coming back up's not easy and with what we got to move, maybe not possible. Also, we want to come out at the bottom by that river down yonder."

He pointed toward what looked, from this height, like a glinting thread, below and off to their right. The thread began in a patch-sized pool at the foot of the cliff, a pool fed by a waterfall that sprang directly from the rock of the cliff face, about a third of the way up from its base.

"The river?" said Mattie. "Why?"

"From here on we got to carry or float that statue," said Cary. "There's variform oak and scrub woods down there such as make a raft that'll float." He looked up at the sky, frowning. "Just hope the weather holds. Rain going down's not good. Slick rock's bad rock to travel. Come on."

He turned and led the way back to the camp. While Mattie had slept the night before, after rousing briefly to eat dinner, Cary had been at work upon the statue and the sledge. He had cut the sledge runners with an ax into rough boards. Then he had bundled the statue in the grass mats and lashed a fence of boards about it on top of the mats, so that the boards would act as fenders on the statue's descent down the cliff face.

With the boards around it now, the statue made a roughly cylindrical bundle that could be rolled along the ground, somewhat clumsily. Using the two axes they had along as pry bars, Cary and Mattie together rolled the statue with only minor difficulty up the slope to the high point from which it fell off sharply to the cliff face. Then, tying an anchor rope around one of the large boulders embedded in the earth at the crown of the slope, Cary assembled sheaves and blocks of the block-and-tackle units among their gear. With these stayed to the anchor line and with Charlie and Mattie, each at an end of the bundle to keep it from slueing around, end on, to the cliff edge below, they cautiously let gravity roll the tethered statue down to the edge.

A half-meter short of the cliff edge, Cary stopped the statue. Leaving it anchored there, he went back for the rest of their gear.

When this was all piled at the cliff edge also, Mattie put on a climbing belt. With another rope snapped to the belt ring, she let herself be lowered by Cary—leaning back and fending herself off from the cliff with her feet as she went down—to the fairly wide ledge of rock six meters below. She unsnapped herself from the line and used it as a guide rope to hold the gear away from the cliff as Cary sent it down on a partnered line, load by load.

When the gear was down, Cary strapped a climbing belt around Charlie's waist, whistling softly and reassuringly to the swamp otter as he worked. Charlie made no audible answer, but the smooth black velvet of his furred throat throbbed with unvoiced whistles; and when Cary first swung him off his webbed feet into the air above the cliff edge, the otter's body and limbs were rigid.

He made no attempt to fend himself off from the cliff on the way down. But Mattie held him clear with the guide rope, as she had protected the loads of gear being sent down. Once on the ledge below, and free of the belt, Charlie burst into a chorus of whistles directed up at Cary.

Cary whistled back shortly and sharply. Charlie's whistling ceased.

"All right, Mattie," Cary called down to her. "Charlie'll help you. Keep that guideline tight so's it doesn't bang the rock."

He anchored the statue by two new lines running from each end of it to the boulder on the crest of the rise behind him. Then, handling the block-and-tackle line himself, he let the bundled statue roll slowly off the edge of the cliff.

"Hold clear, Mattie!" he shouted to her, invisible on the ledge below. He leaned back hard against the block-and-tackle line, letting the statue lower and pause, lower and pause, as he checked it against the end anchor lines and took a fresh grip on the block-and-tackle rope.

After what seemed like a long time, there was a call from Mattie below.

"Almost down! Easy. . . ."

The weight on the block and tackle suddenly ceased, and the line went slack in his hands. Cary straightened up, wiped his forehead with the thumb edge of his hand, and glanced at the sky. It looked hardly changed, but the rents were fewer and farther apart in its cloud cover now.

"Be right down with the ropes and tackle!" he shouted to Mattie. "Make one big bundle of the gear. From now on we got to move some faster."

When he had untied his anchor lines, gathered his block and tackle, and rappelled himself down to join the others, Cary found Mattie had bundled the gear as he had said.

"Fair wrapped," he said, approvingly, looking at the bundle. He stepped over to the rim of the ledge and looked at the one below. "About half again as far down, this time. Hook up, Mattie, and I'll start you down."

This second drop went faster: first because the gear went down in a single bundle, secondly because both Mattie and Charlie now knew what they were to do. On the drops that followed as the day brightened toward noon, they became more practiced. By the time the sun, visible only as a bright area among the clouds, was in its noon position overhead, they had covered more than half the distance to the foot of the cliff. They sat down to a quick, cold meal, the rock slope down which they had come since morning leaning back awesomely above them.

"Pretty good," said Mattie, looking over the rim of the ledge on which they sat. "Looks like the drops are all longer from here. I can see . . . twelve, thirteen . . . fourteen or fifteen more, that's all. Then we'll be able to roll it down that slope at the foot of the edge of that pond where the river starts."

"Sure," said Cary. "But it's going to rain."

She looked up at the now unbroken overcast of the sky.

"You can't be sure," she said. "Clouds are a little darker, that's all."

"Going to rain," said Cary, with finality. He finished eating, peeled off the surface film of his layered plate, and threw the film aside. He put the plate back into the food pack, clean side in.

Mattie gulped the last few bites of bread and dried meat and followed his example. Ten minutes later they were lowering the statue to the ledge below.

But as they went for the ledge below that, there was a cold touch upon the side of Cary's cheek, through his three-day stubble of beard. He said nothing; but when the statue was down safely on the lower ledge, he loosed his anchor lines quickly and rappelled down to join Mattie and Charlie as swiftly as he could.

"Get set to camp," he told Mattie, as his feet touched the barely sloping rock on the ledge.

"Camp?" She stared at him, then held out her hand, palm up. "Just because of a few sprinkles?"

"There'll be more," said Cary. "That rock you're standing on gets mighty slippery, just like it was oiled, after it gets wet enough."

She confronted him.

"But even then," she said, "it's a long way from being wet. We could get down two or three more ledges before a little water like this gets them wet enough to bother. And maybe by that time the rain will have quit."

"Not going to quit," said Cary. "Anyway, look down. Next three, four ledges all got a good slope to their flat—or they're too narrow. No place to camp overnight. Here, the ledge is nice and wide and almost level. Got room for a fire, even."

She opened her mouth.

"No use arguing, Mattie," he said. "You aren't going no place by yourself, without Charlie and me to help you."

She closed her mouth abruptly and turned away to gather up the ropes Cary had let down from the ledge above before coming down himself. Cary turned to search the ledge for small pieces of rock with which to chock the statue bundle against accidentally rolling toward the edge of the drop, three meters away.

As soon as the statue was secure, he set to work to rig a rain shelter flush with the cliff face behind them at one side, so that a patch of the ledge rock would stay dry underfoot. Out beyond the rain shelter he built a fire in the center of the ledge, using pressed fire bricks from among their gear, for the ledge was bare even of moss.

By the time the fire was going well, the first tentative drops of moisture from the cloud-laden sky had become a steady drizzle. This continued steadily throughout the afternoon while they sat idle under the shelter. Charlie lay without moving, his long neck lowered, his head on his right forepaw, staring out and down through the rain at the country below. Cary sat leaning back against some of the piled gear, his eyes closed, half-dozing. From time to time he was roused by the restless sounds of Mattie.

"Might as well settle back, Mattie," he said after a while. "There'll be plenty to do when the time comes for doing."

"At least," her voice came back, sharply, "we could have a breeze around here. There isn't a breath of air stirring."

Cary opened his eyes to see what was disturbing her before he realized it was Charlie's smell. He himself had gotten so used to it that he took it for granted. It was not the acid-musky odor that had come from Charlie earlier when the other swamp otters had roused his anger. This was a fainter, generally fishy stink that was mainly from Charlie's breath. It was not normally too noticeable in the open air; but here under the rain shelter, at close quarters with no air moving, there was no way not to notice it.

"No way Charlie can help it, smelling the way he does," said Cary. "Want to change places with me, Mattie—"

He broke off, catching sight of a silver speck in the far sky below the heavy-bellied clouds, moving steadily to the east.

"What good would that—" Mattie broke off her answer. Glancing over, he saw she had followed his direction of sight and was also watching the silver speck.

"Surveyor craft," she said. "The mortgage people must have it out here mapping."

They watched it out of sight, until it vanished into the overhanging cloud layer itself.

"Cary," said Mattie. He turned and saw her watching him. "Cary, what're you going to do after the new mortgage's voted in?"

He shrugged.

"They'll not be changing times this far upcountry, anyhow," he said. "Not for a while, yet."

"In just a few years. It's all going to be developed, all this—" She gestured at the plateau above and the cliff and the country below. "There'll be roads and cities up here."

"Maybe," said Cary softly. He looked into the fire, burning brightly in spite of the drizzle of drops falling into it. "Be a real fight first, anyway."

"A fight?" Mattie's words pounced on his. "Why a fight? Who'll be fighting?"

"Upcountry people." He looked from the fire to her and found her face tense. "They got guns. They'll fight." He picked up one of the axes and with the metal head prodded the burning brick pieces in the fire together, so that the flame leaped up even more brilliantly. "Won't have no choice, city people and those mortgage misters wanting to change the world all around."

"Violence?" said Mattie. "Violence won't work. If the woodies don't want progress, the only way they can stop it is to turn out down at the city and vote against it. But why should they want to stop progress, anyway? It means a better world for them too."

He shook his head.

"No," he said. "Us people upcountry can't change. Got to die—like the land got to die. Like Arcadia's going to sicken and die from this progress of yours if it comes."

"Die? What're you talking about—die?" The tone of her voice roused Charlie from his gazing and the black head raised on the long neck to look at her. "This world's going to be improved with the mortgage money—not killed."

Cary closed his eyes and relaxed back against the gear.

"Mattie," he said, "don't you ever get tired of arguing?"

"I'm not arguing!" he heard her beyond his closed eyelids. "I'm just trying to talk a little sense, and all I get from you is—there's going to be a fight, the upcountry people're going to die, the land's going to die. You can't kill land."

"Mattie," he answered softly, speaking into the darkness

of his eyelids, "now you know what it is you're doing. You know what I'm talking about; but you want me to say it isn't so, so's you can feel better about it. But what good's my saying, when things're going to happen just the same?"

"I tell you, you can't kill a world! A world's not like a man—or an animal!"

"Sure you can kill a world, Mattie," he said. "All you got to do is level so many mountains, change so many rivers, bring in too many variform trees and such to choke out the native-born stuff like the briar and the thorn bush. All you got to do is plow enough fields, fly enough boats, build enough cities—and you've killed it dead."

"You!" Her voice raged at him. "You talk as if we started here, on Arcadia! It isn't a hundred years since the first people came here to settle. You talk as if we belonged here!"

"Don't take a man more'n a lifetime to belong in the place where he's born," said Cary.

"All right—but then I belong here too! The city people belong just as much on Arcadia as you upcountry woodies."

Eyes still closed, Cary rolled his head from side to side against the gear supporting it from behind.

"Guess you don't though, Mattie," he said. "City people don't belong anywhere—except in any city, on any world, because they're all the same, one city just like another, here on Arcadia. And no reason to think they're different on any other world. Move your city people to some other city, some other planet; it makes no difference."

"That's not true!"

He did not answer. After a while with some sniffs and snorts and some small rustlings around, she also was silent.

When night fell, the fire made its usual curtain of darkness around them, so that they seemed not so much perched on a ledge as enclosed in a roofless room walled in rock and black air. They ate a hot meal this time.

"What about Charlie?" Mattie asked.

Cary glanced at the swamp otter, who lay still, head down, watching them.

"Anywhere there's running water," Cary said, "there's shellfish and waterplant roots like up in the swamp there. And we're going to be following running water, most of the ways. When we're where there's food for him, he'll be able to eat. Otherwise, he's going to have to do without. Can't eat our food."

Sunrise the next morning showed a dark blue sky streaked with high, filmy cirro-stratus clouds. The rock of their ledge was dry outside the rain shelter, and the air was dry and cool.

"Three days of good weather coming anyhow," said Cary, squinting under his palm at the bright sky. "Make the most of it."

They ate a quick breakfast and started the rest of their descent toward the foot of the cliff. Shortly before noon they let the statue bundle down at last on the pebbled slope falling away toward the edge of the waterfall pool. Charlie stayed with Cary and Mattie, impatiently waiting while they rolled the statue down to the edge of the pool. The moment it came to rest by some water grass like that in the plateau swamp, but much taller and thicker-stemmed, the otter plunged into the pool and disappeared.

"He won't go far," said Cary, looking after the otter. "Guess he got pretty dry coming down all that rock. I'll start cutting float logs for the raft. Mattie, you better throw up a camp though. Don't suppose we'll be ready to move on before morn."

He took an ax and strode off through the water grass. A few minutes later Mattie, already busy untying the camping equipment from the gear bundle, heard the distant, steady sound of chopping.

By midafternoon, Cary had cut, rough-trimmed, and dragged to the poolside campsite enough variform oak logs some six to eight inches in diameter to make a raft about three by nine meters in area. He proceeded to tie these logs together with the thin, but extremely strong monomolecular wire he had brought along in the gear. He double-tied each log to the next at both ends, and then laced in and out among the logs and each end with one long strand, which he tightened before tying with a cinch-lever.

Under the pull of the cinch-lever, the fine wire bit into the wood of the logs until it was nearly invisible.

"Look at Charlie," said Mattie.

Cary looked up from completing his last wire tie. Charlie had reappeared at the campsite some time since and had been busy bringing shellfish out of the pool in his mouth. These were bivalves, almost clam-like except for the fact that they were thick enough in the middle to be almost round. Cary had noticed this out of the corner of his eye; but now Mattie's words directed his attention to the fact that, seated in the shallow water at the pool's edge, Charlie was using his forepaws to carefully pat bottom mud from a pile before him around each bivalve, then putting the resultant mudball aside on the shore.

"Charlie, that's not going to work," Cary said. He got to his feet.

Charlie looked up at the sound of his name and watched as Cary came toward him. Cary squatted down beside the otter and whistled intricately, patting the nearest mudball with his hand, pointing to the cliff down which they had

63.

just come and out over the surface of the pond.

"What won't work?" It was Mattie, who had come up behind the man.

Cary got to his feet.

"It's the way they store food for the winter, up in the swamp," Cary said. "He thinks he's going to store food that way for the rest of the trip, in case we're someplace like last night where there's no running water. I can't make him understand."

"Understand what?"

"Up on the plateau, when they do it, it's already turning to cold," Cary said. "The mudballs don't only dry, they freeze. But down here they aren't going to freeze. Those shellfish'll spoil in two days inside mud. But I can't get the notion rightly into him. Well. . . ." Cary turned back toward the raft. "He'll just have to find out for himself."

Left with his shellfish and mudballs, Charlie nosed among them and even picked up some of the mudballs in his raccoon-like paws to handle them puzzledly. Then he abandoned them and went off into the swamp grass. Cary could hear the otter rustling about invisibly in there.

"Now," said Cary to Mattie, recoiling what was left of his monomolecular wire, "we'll lever this into the water to see how she floats—"

A sudden, blindingly bright thread of brilliance reached down from the sky above them into the swamp grass briefly, then disappeared. Charlie whistled piercingly and they heard him thrashing around. Then no more sound, as an amplified voice boomed above them:

"*Look out, down there! There's an animal as big as a bear in that swamp grass right beside you. I got it before it could spring, but maybe it's still alive. Careful! Don't move —I'll be right down and finish it off!*"

64.

6.

Suddenly, many things were happening at once. Cary headed toward the place in the grass from which Charlie's whistle had come. As he went, the fat, teardrop shape of a one-man surveyor craft dropped to earth by the new-made raft, its brilliant white paint and green lettering looking garish against the muted dark tones of the land and vegetation. A slightly overweight, black-haired man in white shirt and blue shorts stepped out.

"Hey!" he called, as Cary brushed by him. "Don't go in there. Maybe it's not dead yet—"

"Better not be dead," said Cary, plunging into the grass. He found Charlie, lying on his side in a little nest of crushed grass. The fur high on one shoulder was still smoking. Charlie lay still, eyes wide open and staring, but when Cary put one hand under a foreleg, the throb of a beating heart pulsed lightly through the rib cage under his palm.

Gently, he picked up the limp, black body and carried it back out to the pile of gear. He laid Charlie down by the gear and jerked a medical kit from the pile. A thick shadow fell across him, and across Charlie.

"What's the matter with you?" The voice of the man from the surveyor craft hammered at him. "I just saved your life,

that's all, and here you go monkeying with that beast as if
—" The voice tone changed as if the man were speaking
off in a new direction. "What's the matter with him, anyway? It's big as a wolf. Look at those teeth. What's he
doing?"

Cary was running a small pair of power surgical clippers
over the burned area to get rid of the hair.

"It's all right, Mattie," he said, putting the clippers aside.
"Far as the burn goes, anyway. Just slid along his side. But
the shock's got him. If he just doesn't go and die from
that—"

"What're you people doing up here, anyway? You don't
act very grateful, either of you. What is it, some sort of pet?
How was I to know? You there—" the voice was aimed
back at Cary again, where he knelt over Charlie. "You
know that's one of the native wild species? I've got every
right to shoot it. I said, *you*! Stand up and answer me when
I talk to you. I'm an interplanetary Senior Survey Officer in
the firm of Eheu and Killey—that's a multiworld outfit,
woodsman! I'd like to know what you're doing here and
what you're doing protecting a wild predator. I think you
better show me your identification—"

Still holding a surgical knife in his hand, Cary got to his
feet and turned as swiftly as the sun blinks behind a fast-
moving cloud. But the Survey Officer was four paces from
him, and Mattie was only a step from the man. Before Cary
could cover the distance, Mattie was between them, her
back to Cary, facing the surveyor.

"*Show you his identification?*" she exploded. "Let's see
your identification, looper! I mean that! Think you've got a
couple of ignorant woodies here you can bully around, do
you? Let me tell you something—I'm Matilda Mary Or-

66.

valo, Orvalo Outfitters of Arcadia City. A citywoman, a native, and a taxpayer. Show me *your* papers!"

"Now look—" the surveyor stared at her, stiff-faced, jaw out-thrust. "I'm a Survey Officer—"

"You!" The word seemed to curdle in Mattie's mouth. "You're a tinker-toy! You're a hired hand for a couple of mortgage contractors who're guests on this world. Guests! And you're not even that. Show *you* his identification? The man you're talking to was born here. He's a citizen, looper. You're nothing! Where's your passport—where's your permit to take native game? Who gave you permission to carry an energy weapon?"

"Nobody said—" the surveyor chewed air furiously.

"That's tough!" said Mattie. "You know why, looper? Because that man here and me, we don't need papers. We were born here. But *you* do. You need a license to breathe —because it's not your air. It's *ours*—understand that? It's *our* air, *our* land, *our* animals, wild or tame. Those two bosses of yours—Eheu and Killey, men so far up in their company they probably never laid eyes on someone like you—they know that, even if you don't. They aren't going to be too happy with an employee who's gone around killing native animals and threatening native citizens, just a couple of weeks before those citizens are due to vote on a five-billion-unit planetary mortgage offered by Eheu and Killey. So you get back in that craft and get your passport and your alien work permit and show them to me, unless you want to leave your flitter here and go back to Arcadia City overland with us in a citizen's arrest!"

Slab-cheeked, pale, and a little wild-eyed, the surveyor backed from her, stumbling, until he came up against the side of his craft.

Without turning, he reached back in through the open doorway, fumbling around.

"And one more thing—" said Mattie. The surveyor froze with his arm in the doorway. She pointed at Cary. "You see that man? You see that short gun at his hip? Well, he can blow your head off with that before you could even get that energy rifle of yours out of that craft. So don't try anything!"

"I wasn't—I wasn't going to—"

"Get those papers, then. Get on with it!"

The surveyor turned about and rummaged hastily inside the doorway. There were the sounds of small objects falling to the metal floor of the craft; then he turned back, holding a small gray booklet and a yellow folder. He brought them to Mattie.

She took them, opened each, and read them through silently and deliberately. Then she handed them back to him.

"Now get out!" she said. "This time we're letting you get away with it. But just keep it in mind from now on. You wanted to know what we're doing here?" She pointed at the wrapped bundle that was the statue. "It just happens we're bringing a very important work of art down to Arcadia City. A statue that's got to be there by the day of the voting —a statue so valuable we wouldn't risk an airboat crashing with it, so we're bringing it down overland. And we're the two *you* wanted to check up on! Go on—get going!"

Carrying passport and permit, he turned back to his craft. As he began to climb in through its doorway, the sound of Mattie's voice brought him to an abrupt halt once more, his back to them.

"And just remember this!" snapped Mattie. "Think of the kind of trouble I could make for you if I went to Eheu and Killey—to the very men themselves—and told them

68.

how you tried to interfere with our bringing that statue in, and the kind of reaction the voters of Arcadia might have if they heard about it!"

She stopped. He stood there for a second or more, his back to them, waiting, then plunged on inside his craft.

The door slammed behind him and the craft jerked up into the air.

"Well, Mattie!" said Cary, looking admiringly at her.

She snorted, evidently still too wound up for compliments.

Suddenly above them the amplified voice blatted down, and looking up, they saw the survey craft hovering some two hundred meters overhead.

"YOU THINK YOU CAN MAKE TROUBLE FOR ME?" it roared, in the surveyor's voice. "WAIT'LL YOU SEE WHAT TROUBLE I CAN MAKE FOR YOU. A FIRM LIKE EHEU AND KILLEY DOESN'T LIKE HICK NATIVES GETTING IN THEIR WAY. YOU WAIT AND SEE!"

Abruptly, the craft went into motion, scooting away into the southwest, in the direction of the coast and Arcadia City, lifting in altitude as it went. Mattie looked after it, the fierceness of her expression slowly changing to a frown.

"I talk too much," she muttered, after a second.

"Wouldn't say that," Cary grinned at her. Her frown remained, though, and he stepped over to touch her lightly and briefly on the shoulder, so that she turned her head from the sky to look at him. "Nothing to worry about. Mister like that's going around asking to be hung all the time. Sooner or later someone's going to take him up on it."

Mattie nodded slowly and relaxed. She even smiled at him, a little.

"I suppose you're right," she said. Her head came up

69.

suddenly and she turned about. "How's Charlie—"

"Leave him be," said Cary, catching her arm as she started toward the otter. Charlie still lay, eyes wide open but unseeing, motionless on his side on the ground where Cary had put him down. A lattice bandage covered the long rectangular area of the shoulder wound from the energy rifle. "It's not the burn. It's shock. Nothing we can do for him now but let him come out of it or not. Up to him."

"Up to him? *Shock?*" She turned on Cary.

"Not regular shock—don't know what else to call it though," Cary said. "His people go that way when things get too much for them. You know how it's been—him getting hooted out of the swamp by his own relatives, then coming down that mountain. Now, out of nowhere, he gets shot like that, with no way to see it coming, no way to dodge, no way of knowing what it was for. So, he's gone like this. He'll come out of it or he'll die, one of the two. But nothing we can do about it."

Mattie stared at the unmoving black form.

"How do you know he'll come out of it?" she asked, in a surprisingly hushed voice.

"Seen his people like this before. Seen him this way once before, too, after he saved my life. I told you that."

Mattie turned to look up at him.

"No, you didn't," she said. "You never said anything about his being like this."

"Didn't I? Maybe not, then," said Cary. "I told you how come he saved me? How I was sick with blood poisoning but running my trapline anyway?"

She nodded.

"And I caught an otter in one of my traps—dead she was by that time," Cary said. "And the whole tribe

70.

swarmed me when I folded up, trying to get the body out of the trap. It was Charlie's mate."

"You told me that," Mattie said. "You said the others wanted to kill you, but he made them keep you alive so that he could try to find out why you wanted to kill them, so maybe they could stop the killing."

"Sure," said Cary. "It was after the others promised not to kill me, he passed out like this." He shook his head slowly, remembering. "You know, Mattie, for a long time I thought it was his mate being killed that made him fold up, but he held off long enough to save my life first. But that wasn't right. I got to know his people some better, then I understood."

"It wasn't his mate?"

"Oh, sure it was that too," said Cary. "But what I mean is, that was just part of it. Truth is, they don't have any real control over passing out like this. Part of what did it to him then was losing his mate—they only match up once a lifetime, you know—but the other part was me. You saw how the others don't have much use for him. The only reason they gave in to him about me was because it was his mate I'd killed. So, all of a sudden there he was, not only with his mate dead, but with a sick, two-legged trapper to care for and all the responsibility to the rest of the tribe for keeping me alive."

Cary laughed suddenly, one of his rare, soundless laughs.

"You know—it was me, sick as I was, who tried to take care of him? Instead of him, me? Until he came to; and I really folded up, of course."

"Did you really know he'd saved your life then?" Mattie asked. She was looking at him penetratingly.

"Why sure," said Cary. "Maybe I couldn't whistle-talk

71.

with them then—I can't really now, for that matter. But I was pretty well conscious through the whole thing. When a gang of black demons with teeth as long as your middle finger start dancing all around you and taking nips, and another black demon jumps up on your chest and whistles at the rest until they all back off, after a big hullabaloo—you get the idea. True. Fact is, when I first passed out and came to for a bit to see him lying there like he is now, I thought his people'd come back and killed him for backing me up."

"You keep saying you can't hardly talk to him," Mattie said. "Seems to me you understand him pretty well."

"Well, that's right enough," said Cary. "But it's not so much from talk, or sign language, or anything. You just get to know a person after a while, and you pick up a lot of stuff about him without him having to tell you."

He stopped talking and gazed at Charlie for a moment.

"Nothing to do but wait," he said. "Morn'll bring us the answer, one way or other. Meanwhile, you and I can get that raft floated and loaded right and everything ready for downriver."

They woke next morning to a warm and cloudless day and the white, dead ashes of the campfire. Beyond the fire, where Charlie had lain, the ground was empty. Cary climbed out of his sleeping hammock and saw Mattie, still in hers, her eyes on him.

"Nothing to do with me, if that's what you're thinking," Cary said. "I didn't get up in the night and put him somewheres else. He's come to on his own and gone off a bit, that's all."

In fact, before breakfast was fairly started, the waters of the pool parted to reveal the head of Charlie, carrying in another bivalve shellfish in his mouth. He climbed out of the water with it, sat down by his mudpile, and started covering the mollusk with the mud.

Cary whistled to him.

"Let's look at that shoulder, Charlie," he said

Charlie finished mudballing his shellfish and came up to Cary.

"Good enough," said Cary, examining the wound. He patted the bandage back in place. "No inflammation, hardly. Never tell how a native animal's going to take doctoring. Right; we'll load what's left and travel."

They finished breakfast, got the rest of their gear aboard, including Charlie's mudballed shellfish, and floated the raft, which they had loaded with the statue and dragged into the shallow water at the pool's edge the night before. The raft rode evenly; the statue, still in its wrappings of rope and ax-trimmed boards, lay a little to the rear to counterbalance the weight of the pile of gear up front.

"On our way," said Cary.

They poled across the pond, then had to get off and half-drag, half-push the raft through the shallow water where the pool spilled out to begin the stream. Once past this, the raft floated well again, with Cary and Mattie aboard. Charlie swam alongside for perhaps the first half-mile or so downstream, then climbed aboard and lay in the sun, occasionally examining the bandage on his shoulder with his nose and delicate touchings with his teeth.

"You think there's something wrong with that bandage?" asked Mattie, watching the otter, the tenth or eleventh time he did this.

Cary shook his head.

"Just itching him probably," Cary said. "I'll look at it again at noon, or after."

By noon, the character of the mountain stream they were following had changed markedly. From a slow, meandering thread of water in spots hardly deep enough to float a raft, it had increased in average depth to nearly a meter and had widened to perhaps thirty meters. It was now taking a more direct route down the slope of the mountainside. The current was fast and the water mounded up as it passed over submerged boulders, or broke into swollen collars of foam and turbulence around large, half-submerged boulders.

Mattie stood at the back, holding a steering oar made of two ax-trimmed boards wired to a long pole fastened between a pair of upright pegs in the end of the center log. Cary rode up front with his pole to fend them off from the black, gray, and darkly reddish-brown boulders rearing like granite trolls out of the swiftly swirling water. Charlie, although he seemed tempted to get into the water less than a meter from him, lay on the deck by the statue, nosing its boards and ropes from time to time.

The river widened further and increased its pace. The roar of its waters was like a wall around them now, and the spray thrown up from the water-assaulted boulders at times hid the clumps of briar and variform oak on the rocky shores. A faint sound began to worry Cary, demanding his attention, and after a second, he realized it was Mattie shouting to him from the back end of the raft.

He turned his head.

"What?" he called.

"Can't we slow down a bit?" her voice came to him, thin and thready amid the steady water sounds, which did not seem that loud, but which muted everything else. "I can hardly steer it!"

He frowned and shook his head at her.

"River's higher'n I figured!" he shouted back. "Water get's

even faster the next three klicks or so. Tie yourself to something, so you don't slip off—and stick with that oar!"

She nodded, saving her breath apparently; and he turned back to his poling. Just in time, for a reddish boulder the size of ten statues was looming before them, all but dead in the path of the raft.

As he had predicted, the waters increased their speed. The raft was not into real rapids, even now, but it leaped and plunged among the boulders like an ox unbroken to saddle or harness. Once again, Cary got the small, irritating feeling that Mattie was calling to him; but he could not turn around now, with boulders appearing in front of him in every direction. Then the raft's front end was lifted over a drowned boulder from which Cary had not been able to pole them clear. It pitched up at an angle—

And a scream brought Cary whirling about.

Behind him, dwindling in the distance, the statue, half of its boards and matting knocked away, sat in the river, propped half-upright against the boulder. Mattie clung to the statue, and he heard her scream again. Bits of ax-hewn board and matting were strewing themselves along the stream below the statue. The black head of Charlie bobbed in the water by the boulder.

The raft grated on another boulder and lurched sideways. Cary spun back to look ahead of him and got his pole out just in time to fend them off from a square chunk of black rock like a closed door in the way. His eyes ranged ahead. Just a hundred meters farther on the river bent to the right, and the inner side of the curve, behind a fence of riverbed boulders, had a patch of calm and open water touching on an open bank.

Cary reached out with the pole and thrust hard, trying to swing the raft in toward the open patch.

For a moment there was no reaction. Then, caught by a spinning current, the raft began to revolve, end for end. Once more Cary heaved desperately on his pole—and the raft, by now level with the upper rocks of the fence of boulders, tried to go through sideways between two of them. It slammed hard against the lower of the two boulders, and rode at last into the slower, open water.

Cary poled the raft to the bank. The current pushed strongly against it, holding it halfway up the small slope of the level earth beyond.

He snatched up a length of rope that was anchored in a cleat nailed to the center log. He jumped ashore carrying the rope and found a briar tree up on the level ground to tie the raft to. Then, finally, he could take time to look back upriver.

There was nothing to see. Mattie was back up around the bend of the watercourse and out of sight. Cary leaped down to the raft and rummaged through the gear, coming up with ax, rope, light line, and a block and tackle. Ax in hand, and with the other items tied to his belt or hooked onto his clothing, he began to lope back upstream along the bank.

Bushes impeded his passage. Several times he was forced to go down the bank and wade in the shallow water at the river's edge to get by clumps of trees or vines. But finally he saw Mattie up ahead, still clinging to the half-submerged statue in the middle of the tumbling river, with the black otter head of Charlie holding station in the waters just downstream of her.

He reached the shore opposite her, leaned against the trunk of a taup tree for a moment to get his breath, and then tried to call her.

But plainly she could not hear him over the noise of the river. She continued to stare downstream. He whistled, and Charlie's head turned toward the shore. A second later the head was parting the water strongly, swimming toward him. Within a couple of minutes, Charlie hauled himself, dripping, up onto the bank.

Looking out at Mattie again, Cary saw that she, too, was now looking shoreward. Evidently she had watched Charlie's swim to shore. Cary waved to her. She did not let go of the statue in order to wave back; but she nodded her head violently, and he could see her lips moving. But it was impossible to hear whatever she was saying.

Cary made one end of the light line fast to the rope and fitted the rope into the block and tackle. He held out the other end to Charlie, who took it in his mouth. Cary pointed to Mattie, clinging to the statue with the foam-flecked water plucking at her legs.

"Okay, Charlie," Cary said.

The swamp otter turned and went smoothly once more into the river current. He seemed to move almost without effort at right angles to the rushing current, but Cary noted that the black head pointed, not straight across the river, but at an angle upriver as it progressed.

Charlie reached the statue and Mattie grudgingly loosened the grip of her right arm around the carved rock to take the end of the line from Charlie's mouth. With both arms still around the statue, she stared at Cary, ashore. He made pulling motions with his arms, as if hauling in something on a long tether.

Her head went up and down, nodding. She began slowly drawing the light line in to her, letting the pulled-in part trail behind her in the water. The head of the rope to which

Cary had attached the line lifted from the bank and began to curve its way against the current through the water to her.

It reached her at last. She looked at Cary. He made the motions of tying off the rope around the narrow part of the statue that was its waist. She struggled to obey, once losing her grip on the statue and sliding halfway down into the water before she climbed back up to finish the job. When she was done, she nodded vigorously to Cary.

Cary anchored the block and tackle to the trunk of a heavy variform oak and used the tackle to pull the rope taut. He locked the sheaves of the block and tackle. Then, holding the now-tight rope stretching between tree and statue, he inched slowly into the river.

For the first third of the distance, he kept his feet under him with the help of the rope. Then he stepped down into a place where the water was waist deep, and his legs went from under him. For a moment, he felt that the current would pull him from the rope in spite of anything he could do. Then fury boiled up in him. He pulled himself back above the rope like a man chinning himself on a bar. Suddenly he felt assistance, something pushing his legs back and down against the pressure of the water.

It was Charlie, swimming strongly and pressing against Cary's lower body. Cary got his legs on the riverbed once more and went back to working his way out to the statue. After a while he reached it and looked up to see Mattie, wet hair hanging around her face, looking down at him.

"You all right, Mattie?" he shouted.

She nodded.

"Easy, then," he said. "All you got to do is get down into the water behind me and keep hold of the rope with your hands outside my hands. We'll go back together."

She nodded. Her face was as white as if there were no blood left in her; but she let herself down into the water behind him and reached around him with her right arm to take hold of the rope beyond him.

With the river pressing her weight against him, Cary's feet started to leave the bottom again. Pressure from Charlie's black body held them there. All three together, fighting the river as they inched with great effort toward the shore.

When they got into shallow enough water so that Cary and Mattie could hold their feet down by themselves, Charlie abandoned them. He swam into the bank, pulled himself up its small slope onto level ground, and abruptly lay still, neck outstretched.

Minutes later, Cary and Mattie blundered up the bank and also collapsed. Cary lay only a few seconds, however, before rousing himself to move over and inspect Charlie.

"Bandage gone," he said, looking over at Mattie, who lay exhausted on the ground, watching him. "He's wore out too, of course; but that's all. Didn't do himself any real hurt on top of what he had, seems to me."

He got creakily to his feet.

"I'll go see about moving the raft up here," he said, and went off down along the shoreline. However, not a hundred meters from where he had left Mattie and Charlie, his legs began to tremble, and his knees folded up under him like frozen lengths of rope thawed by a campfire.

Kneeling, slumped on the ground, he looked at his legs.

"Well," he said to them, "you could have let me down earlier, and you didn't. I'm beholding to you for that."

7.

There was no hope of getting back on the river that day. Cary had to spend several hours working the raft back up along the shoreline against the current, anchoring it to one tree, and then hauling it by block and tackle up to a new anchor point where it could be tied off and the whole procedure repeated. For the last hour or so, Mattie came and worked with him. But Charlie lay where he had stopped after climbing out of the water, and he had not moved by the time they finally brought the raft up level with the statue and anchored it to the bank under the taut rope curving out to the tooth-carved stone.

There were still a couple of hours of daylight left. Cary fitted a new bandage on Charlie and then set about hauling the statue in to shore. Under the pull of the rope the statue toppled slowly sideways and vanished under the surface of the river. Charlie came to his feet. He ran down the slope, plunged into the water, and headed out to where the rope vanished into the swirling current. But less than a third of the way out he slowed, turned, and swam slowly back to shore. He climbed the bank, his head held low and wagging on his long neck as if he was shaking it to himself over the situation. He dropped down at full length on the ground once more, to lie with his throat throbbing with unvoiced whistles, watching Cary at work.

The statue was more stubborn an object to move than even the raft. Four times it got caught on boulders underwater on the way to shore; and four times Cary had to wade out and lever it free, fighting current, pole, and statue all at once. But just before sunset it was finally dragged to the river's edge, and Cary levered it aboard the raft, grounded in the bankside shallows.

It was dark before their meal was over. The food and the sudden end to the need to keep himself moving and working operated on Cary like the effects of some heavy sedative. He sat propped against a pile of gear, legs stretched out, eyelids heavy, barely able to keep awake enough to finish the second cup of strong coffee in his hand.

His body felt limp and useless as an unraveled string. Clouds had moved in with the sunset. There was no light overhead and no moon on the river, which roared by unseen except for the small patch of shallows where the raft with the statue upon it lay touched by illumination from their campfire. The flickering light and shadow upon the statue seemed to make it move like a live thing, seemed to give a living expression to its face. Cary found himself, with Mattie, sitting and staring at it.

"You know, Cary," Mattie said, soberly, "I almost drowned for the sake of that thing there, today."

Cary nodded heavily and roused himself to answer.

"Two thousand units's a lot of money, Mattie."

She scowled.

"Yes," she said. "But it's more than just the units—ever since that surveyor early today. That crim looper! I'd bring that statue in now just to set it up in the public park of Arcadia City, even if your art dealer wasn't paying a script dollar for it!"

Cary opened his eyes more widely and gazed at her.

"Would you, Mattie?" he said.

"You heard what I said!" she retorted, but there was less heat to her voice than the words signaled. She gazed at the statue for a moment without saying anything. "Charlie was worried too, wasn't he?"

She looked over at Cary.

"It was the statue, really, that made him go into the river and help us, wasn't it—and he wasn't actually up to it. Remember how he tried to swim back out to the statue when we started to drag it ashore and he couldn't make it? But before that, he'd helped you save me. Only, it wasn't so much for me he did it, was it? It was so the statue'd get saved?"

Cary nodded slowly.

"I guess he'd have tried to help anyway, Mattie," he said. "Maybe not so hard though." Cary watched her. "Can't blame him, you know, for thinking a lot of that statue. He's put out a lot for it, first to get it made, and now to get it this far. All he wants is to see it someplace where people'll want to come look at it."

"They will too," said Mattie. She was watching the statue in the dancing firelight again. "You know, I didn't really look it over back up in the swamp when you first showed it to me. All it seemed to me then was a stone with just a few little angles to it that made it look like a standing man with a long gun. The light's a lot worse here, but I can see better. I can almost make out the expression on your face—or the statue's face. Because it's you, all right—only, you know, it's something else too. It's you, but then at the same time it's like every woodie I've ever seen come into Orvalo Outfitters. You know what I mean?"

She turned to him.

Cary shook his head above the coffee cup.

"Looks just like me, to me," he said.

"You aren't looking at it the right way," said Mattie. "There's something big about it that's like you, all right— but it's like something more than you at the same time. There's something about it as if it was still standing with its lower end in the earth—like you couldn't ever take it out of the earth. Like it was protecting the earth. . . . You can't see that?"

Cary lifted his head and squinted at the statue through grainy eyes.

"Looks like me saying I own something, all right," he said, after a moment.

"No! *More* than that." She was frowning at him. "More than you, don't you see . . . ? What do you see in it, anyway? Tell me how it looks to you."

Cary took a deep breath and tried hard to focus on the statue in the shifting firelight.

"Well, it's me—just the way I say," he answered. "That's my old long gun I'm holding ready—the one that got lost in the mudhole, not this one here. I got my heavy leathers on, because it's late fall and you can see how the mud's frozen in clumps, like high on my boots. I got my short gun slung forward where I can get at it, but the flap's still down to keep the sleet off it. Same time, I got no gloves on; and you can see how I'm holding my hands back against my jacket front to help keep my fingers from getting too cold and stiff in the wind. There's the knife in my boot top and a light pack on my back. . . ."

Heat burned his right leg suddenly, and he jerked upright out of a half-doze into which his own voice had tricked him, to discover the cup fallen from his hand and coffee spilled on the leg below. Then he was so exhausted his head spun. Out of the spinning he became aware of the face of Mattie only a few inches in front of him. His vision cleared. She was holding the now empty cup and rubbing his damp leg with a corner of a sleeping bag liner.

"But you see even more than I do. . . ." Her eyes glowed strangely at him. There was an odd expression on her face. "No, don't try to talk about it now. You're out on your feet. Here's your bag—slide into it." Clumsily, he obeyed and found himself horizontal on the ground, the sleeping bag warming around him, the firelight making rapid changes of expression on Mattie's face—framed by her darkly hanging hair—and floating above him.

"Sleep. . . ." she said.

"Maybe. . . ." he began. And suddenly he realized he did not know what he had been going to say. Before he could remember, slumber took him.

He came awake, hardly realizing he was doing so, some time later in the night. He rose and propped himself on one elbow to look about the campsite.

Mattie lay sleeping on her side in her bag on the hammock. The fire was down to little trickling flames and glowing coals. Beyond the fire, Charlie lay, head down but eyes open and bright with reflection from the firelight, silently watching Cary. There was a sleeping bag liner to one side of the swamp otter, which looked as if it had been covering him but had been pulled off or shrugged aside. Beyond, the unseen river roared unceasingly, open-throated, but seemingly muted now, because of the familiarity of its voice.

Cary slid out of the bag and got quietly to his feet. As

Charlie's eyes watched him, he stepped over to add fresh wood chunks to the fire.

As the flames licked up on the new fuel, Cary straightened up and stepped further on, to stand by the side of Mattie's hammock, looking down at her face. Her hair had recovered from the straightness of its wetting in the river. It had been brushed back into soft waves and her face was clean. The fingertips of one hand, showing above the edge of the sleeping bag, up by her face, were clean, with no dirt showing under the nails.

Cary turned and held his own hand up to the firelight. It showed darkly there with tan and ingrained soil. The nails were jet black in semicircles under their ends. He ran a hand over his jaw and the wire-stiff bristles of a six-day beard scratched thickly at his palm.

He turned away from Mattie. Charlie's eyes still watched him. Cary went over and squatted by the swamp otter, placing his hand lightly on the black shoulder above the line of white bandage. Under the velvet-soft fur, the shoulder was hot.

Cary got to his feet, went to the gear, and came back with another bandage, which he spread out as he walked until it was like a small, thick blanket about the area of a table napkin. He went on past Charlie down to the edge of the river. He dipped the bandage into the water and held it there until it had been soaked by the cold stream. Then he brought it back and spread it all over the bandaged shoulder.

Charlie lifted his head briefly from the ground to look at it and then laid his head back down again, watching Cary. A small whistle warbled in his throat.

Cary rose and went to the pile of gear again. This time he rummaged out soap, solvent, and a self-sharpening razor. He carried these down and squatted by the water's edge.

Charlie whistled softly behind him.

Cary got to his feet, leaving on the bank the things he had brought, and went back to the otter. Carefully, he picked up Charlie and carried him to the raft, laying him down on its inner edge. Charlie whistled again. Reaching back with his supple neck, he took the wet, unfolded bandage in his teeth, dipped it in the running water between raft and shore, then laid it back up on his shoulder.

"Should've thought of it earlier," Cary said to him, squatting once more by the river edge.

Cary dampened his face with the cold water, dipped one end of the soap in the stream, held it there for a second, and then scrubbed the softened end of the soap into his beard. When it was thickly coated, he took the razor and began to shave while Charlie watched, occasionally giving little whistles like soft questions. Cary did not answer.

When the beard was gone, Cary stripped off his jacket and shirt and began to wash his arms and upper body. He soaped and rubbed his clothes in the running water, with the firelight flickering redly upon him, the river roaring by invisibly, and Charlie watching.

In the morning he was up before Mattie, wearing clothes not yet quite dry that steamed before the fire as he fixed breakfast over the wick-stove. He looked up from this after a bit to see Mattie awake in her hammock, staring hard at him.

"Morn," he said.

"Morning," she answered. She looked at him for a moment longer. Her face changed as if she was about to say something—then changed again. She got out of the hammock without a word and went past him into the bushes, saying over her shoulder, "Breakfast ready? Good. I'll be there in a minute."

Later on, with the food eaten, and as they were finishing their coffee, she spoke to him in a lowered voice.

"Charlie's worse, isn't he?"

"Feverish-like all around that place he was shot," Cary answered. "Don't know how bad that means it's getting. Maybe it's just natural, his heating up like that."

"Don't you know?" she asked. "You must've seen his people when they were hurt, before this."

"Hurt, sure," he said. "Cuts, bites, scrapes, feet frozen —even bullets in them. Never seen one burned, though. Nothing up there on the plateau to burn any of them, 'less he walked into a fire, and he'd know better'n that. He feels better with a wet bandage on it, so I fixed him up."

She nodded slowly.

"He better not move around any, though," she said. "Nothing that's sick or hurt gets better unless it can rest. He won't have to leave the raft today, will he?"

"Guess he will," said Cary. "Not more than an hour downstream we come to Apfur's stock station. Mister there named Aige Apfur's got a store and some harness-broke cattle. We'll need to leave the raft there, hire a couple oxen, and then travois cross-plains to the Strike River. Strike River runs all the way down to the farmlands by Arcadia City. This stream don't."

"What's travois?"

"Travois—that's what they call a drag cart. You'll see." Cary got to his feet. "Not as easy riding as the raft, but it'll carry Charlie and the statue overland to the Strike. We'd best start packing."

The sun was barely into the upper branches of the oaks along the river when the stream broadened out and became tranquil. Just around a further bend they came upon a clearing with a large log building with a porch under a vine roof sitting well back from the river. Alongside the building was a pole corral holding a number of variform cattle—short-bodied, deeper-chested and more nimble-legged than the domestic Earth-native strain from which they had been derived.

There seemed no one in sight when they came around the bend, though a curl of gray smoke was coming out a stone chimney at one end of the building. But by the time Cary had poled the raft into the bank below the building there were five men coming down to meet them.

The one in the lead wore bush pants and a heavy up-country shirt under a leather jacket, a city-processed one with a slick exterior. He was a short, broad, brown-faced man with very white teeth. The other four were pale-skinned men, dressed in white dirt-resistant static shirts and blue shorts with the EK symbol of the mortgage contractors' firm overlaid in gold on the right leg of each pair of shorts. The faint gold glow of a weather shield surrounded each of them.

"Loopers," muttered Mattie.

Cary did not bother to answer. For the fact that the four were interlopers was written as plainly on them as it had been on the surveyor earlier. Those skins and clothes had never originated on Arcadia. As they stepped ashore from the raft, Cary could see to the right and behind the log building a pair of white plastic igloos, also with the Eheu and Killey symbol in gold on their dome roofs.

"Aige," said Cary, as the brown-faced man in local clothes reached the raft first. He nodded at the man.

"Cary. And I don't know the missus—" began Aige Apfur, turning to Mattie. But Mattie broke in sharply.

"Miss. Matilda Mary Orvalo. Orvalo Outfitters, Arcadia City."

"Orvalo Outfitters?" Aige grinned. "That'll be Dave Orvalo—"

"My father," said Mattie, with a snap. "Dead seven years ago."

"Why—regrets." Aige's grin sobered. "And your mother—"

"Dead three years after that. No need for courtesies, Mister Apfur. I'm Orvalo Outfitters now, and we've got some business to do with you."

She looked unfavorably past him at the four loopers who had by now reached the river bank beside him and were examining the statue and Charlie with some amusement.

"Why, glad to," said Aige. "Used to do business with Dave, once upon a time—"

"And you paid for what you got?" said Mattie.

"Paid?" Aige stared. "Why sure, Miss Orvalo. I always did business cash."

"No offense, Mister Apfur," said Mattie, stepping ashore. "It was a weakness of my father's—doing business with people who didn't pay for what they got. I believe in cash myself, just like you; so we'll have no trouble." She turned to Cary, still on the raft. "What'd you say we'd need from Mister Apfur?"

"Travois," said Cary. "Couple of drawing oxen. Leave you the raft here, Aige, for what it's worth."

"For what it's worth, Mister Apfur," said Mattie. "Even a raft's got worth."

"Why, sure," said Aige. "We'll figure that in, of course.

Cary, there's maybe half a dozen travois, all sizes, around back of the house. Whyn't you pick one out and the oxen you want from the corral and load up. I'll take Miss Orvalo up to the house for a cup of coffee. When you're done, we can come back out, see what you picked, and figure our deal."

"Maybe I'd better stay here," said Mattie, looking sourly at the loopers, who had been muttering and laughing among themselves, and showing a tendency to crowd around the statue and Charlie on the raft. "Unless these gentlemen can be trusted not to touch anything."

"You don't need to worry about us, Orv—Miss Orvalo, is it?" a lean, middle-aged looper with receding hair said to her. "We're just getting a kick out of the whole thing. You must be the people sent old Sam Moroy scooting back to the City as if you'd set his pants on fire. It was you, wasn't it? This the statue?"

"It's the statue we're taking overland down to Arcadia City," said Mattie. "Valuable property."

"Why sure—sure. You know workingmen like us don't know a lot about art. Could have been just any old rock for all we could tell. . . ." The other loopers began to grin. "No, no. Cut that out, Team."

The grins vanished from the faces of the other three.

"You've got to forgive us, Miss Orvalo," said the lean looper. "We all know Sam, and it was the funniest thing we ever heard, the way you told him off, and the way he went sailing down to the City to tell his tale about you. I'm Harby Wiles—Jeth Horogh, Noyal Penz, Mace Droy." The other three nodded to Mattie as they were introduced. "Now, we won't touch a thing. We'll come up to Aige's place there, and have a cup of coffee with you; and you can tell

90.

us how it really was when you set fire to old Sam's tail that way."

The four men and Mattie went up the sloping bank to the combination store and house that Aige Apfur owned. They mounted the steps, crossed the narrow porch, and disappeared inside. Left alone, Cary walked up the slope, around the house, and examined a row of travois leaning against the log wall.

These were light, long, odd-looking vehicles made of two bire tree trunks with some of the heavy, curved roots still attached. They were stripped of skin and limbs and joined together at the top end to a harness-bearing yoke for two drawing beasts. From that joining, the two tree trunks spread out at a forty-degree angle, with the polished, tough, curved roots resting curve down on the ground. Extending from near the joined tops almost to the roots, the two trunks were joined by board slats to make a flat bed.

Cary picked out the larger of these, a travois nearly five meters from yoke to roots. Getting between it and the log wall, he lifted its yoke end from the wall, swiveled the travois around on its roots, and laid it down flat to examine it. The slats were firm and well nailed, and the bearing yoke was a single S-shaped pad of steamed wood, padded generously with leather underneath. When Cary stood on the roots of both tree trunks, one at a time to test them, they had good spring in them yet.

There was a harness spike-punch, like a wooden-handled ice pick stuck into the log wall by the end of the row of travois. Cary pulled it loose and used the sharp metal point to probe the leather underside of the yoke. The leather was soft and new and was firmly glued to the wood above it over all its connecting surface.

He left the travois where he had laid it and went down to the pole corral. Taking halters from the top pole of one of the sections, he let himself in and set about the business of first choosing, then capturing the variform oxen he had picked for the trip to the Strike River.

Ten minutes later the pair of oxen he had picked were outside the corral and yoked to the travois. He led the beasts down to the raft, trailing the travois with the up-curved roots bumping and sliding over the ground behind them.

He backed the travois up to the edge of the raft where it was grounded at the river's edge, and whistled Charlie from the statue. While the variform oxen stood patiently, he levered the statue around so that it would be headed end up on the travois, and then he put a rope about its head. Latching a block and tackle to the crown point of the bearing yoke between the two beasts, he slowly drew the statue up onto the slats of the travois, locked the block and tackle, and tied the statue in place.

Charlie, making little whistles in his throat, crept off the raft and up onto the travois, until he lay once more on top of the statue.

Cary loaded the rest of the gear onto the travois and tied it securely in position. Then he stood back. The two oxen bore the weight of the joined top end of the supporting trunks upon their bearing yoke with complacency. Cary nodded to himself, led the oxen up between the house and the hotel, and tethered them to a ground stake there.

Mattie and the men were still inside the log building. Cary went in and found them sitting around the store section at the front—a large, open room piled high with gear and food supplies. Mattie and the men were sitting among the stacked blankets with coffee cups in their hands. The smell of something more than sugar in their coffee perfumed the still air.

"All set," said Cary, briefly to Mattie and Aige. "Want to come outside and look it over?"

"Don't rush there!" called the lean looper named Harby Wiles, from his seat on a counter beside a pile of import equipment, four energy rifles, and other gear that obviously belonged to him and his companions. Wiles reached over to a stand beside the counter on which a coffee maker stood, and filled a cup. "Taste some import coffee, friend. Want it royale?"

"Which, mister?" asked Cary.

"With booze in it—booze," said Wiles, reaching into the pile beside him for a large white flask from which he poured a brown stream into the fresh cup of coffee. He poured generously. Cary was conscious of Mattie's eyes on him, but she said nothing. Cary's woods-sensitive nose caught the same smell of liquor coming from her own coffee cup.

"There you are, friend," said Wiles, passing the cup into Cary's hands. "Coffee and import booze such as you never tasted before. Drink happy." He slid off the counter and headed for the front door. "Excuse me, folks. Be right back."

He went out. Cary tasted the liquor-laced coffee. It did not taste as powerful as he had expected, seeing the amount Wiles had poured into the cup. Cary sipped it carefully. There was a long day of travois ahead. Take it down slow and it wouldn't slow him up as much.

"Poor old Sam," one of the other loopers went on. As Cary remembered, it was the one called Mace something, a short young man with a big-boned face. "Never seen him so peeled off. He was bound and determined to get right back to headquarters at your Arcadia City and start blackening your reputations—"

"That reminds me," Mattie interrupted, turning to Aige, "you wouldn't have a radiophone here I could use to call down to the City?"

"Sorry, miss." Aige shook his head, apologizing with a flash of white teeth. "Parts cost too much. Just an airboat in once a month. It's due in tomorrow though. Want me to send a message?"

Mattie shook her head.

"No. Never mind." She turned back to Mace. "Didn't mean to interrupt. Go on."

"Well," said Mace, "I was just telling you all. Sam was bound to spread a story that'd get you into plenty trouble with E and K—you know, the big boys." He winked. "So, just before he took off, he was asking us all what ought to be done about you two—"

A shrill swamp-otter whistle from outside the building sounded through the log walls as if they had been made of woven swamp grass.

8.

Cary dropped his cup, spun about, and made it to the door in three long strides. He jerked the door open and was through it, running along the porch toward the corner behind which he had left the travois, while the reverberations of that single piercing whistle were still making his ears sing.

He leaped off the porch, turned the corner of the building, and confronted the lean looper, Wiles. Wiles was standing over the statue on the travois, a sledgehammer still held upraised in his hands. His shirt was torn open, and one leg of his shorts was torn and flapping. Charlie lay beside the travois, half on his back, his neck outstretched and his eyes closed, his teeth half-grinning between his lips. His body quivered slightly and occasionally, like the body of a sleeping dog. Dark blood welled slowly from the fur on the right side of his head.

At the sight of Cary, Wiles dropped the sledgehammer and snatched up Cary's own long gun, which lay on top of the gear lashed to the travois.

"Hold it!" said Wiles. His face twisted. "Just hold it. That's right. Unhook that gunbelt around you and let it drop. Now back off four steps."

Slowly, Cary obeyed. The belt with his short gun in its holster thudded to the hard dirt at his feet. He backed.

"That damn beast of yours went for me," said Wiles, grinning a little now. He raised his voice. "Hey, Team! Get the woman out here—oh, there you are."

Cary moved his eyes without moving his head. Mattie came around the building, followed by the three other loopers, all now carrying energy rifles. Aige walked with them. They came back and stopped.

Cary looked down at Charlie, lying bleeding and quivering on the ground, then back up to Wiles.

"You're dead, mister," he said.

Wiles laughed.

"No. *You're* dead, woodie," he said. "That is, unless we decide to be generous and let you go, in about a week from now." He looked over at Mace. "Did you explain things to them, Mace?"

"I'd just got as far as Sam asking us for advice about what to do when the animal whistled," Mace said.

"Well, that's good enough." Wiles turned back to Cary. "That's right, Sam asked us for advice. And we told him— go on in and spread his story about, but we'd handle it up here for him, just to make sure."

He smiled.

"You know what I told Sam about you?" he went on. "I said you aren't the first smart local hick to give a company man trouble. Lots of time the Team has trouble with some native or other on an outback world like this. We're used to it. And we like to handle it ourselves without getting the company moneymen involved. The moneymen like it that way too—"

"What do you think's going to happen with your moneymen when they hear about this?" interrupted Mattie

96.

fiercely. "With an election coming up and a mortgage worth billions up for vote—"

"But they aren't going to hear about it," Wiles interrupted in his turn. "That's the line you used on old Sam, wasn't it? But there's a simple answer. E and K might worry about this a bit if they heard of it before the voting. But once the mortgage's voted, they're not going to give two hells. Because by that time they'll have the signatures of enough citizens on the dotted line, and it'll be all over, lady. In fact, once they get the mortgage in their pocket, they'll be just as glad we instilled a little respect in you hicks."

"Only," said Mattie, savagely, "they're going to hear about it before the voting, just as soon as we get to town."

"You aren't getting to town," said Wiles. "We'll just stash you away someplace with one of the Team to guard you until the voting's over. Then, if you've been real nice people all the while, maybe we'll even just turn you loose. Of course, we'll skin your beast here, and crack up this statue thing of yours, just to teach you a little lesson—but that's not all that bad, is it? As long as you come out of it alive?"

Cary looked at Aige, standing behind the men with the rifles by the end of the tall row of travois leaning against the log wall.

"Aige," he said.

"That's right—I was forgetting Aige." Wiles looked over at the store owner. "You've got a stake in this too, Aige, you know. You wouldn't want a couple like these two here getting down to Arcadia and stirring up trouble that might somehow get in the way of this world's new mortgage, would you? I'd imagine a man like you is planning to buy into half a dozen of the subsidiary companies that'll be growing up after the mortgage."

Aige grinned and backed up against the log wall beside the first of the racked travois.

"Well, that's a fact," he said. "I've been saving for years here for a chance to make a little money. Sure, I have."

His grin widened. He leaned his shoulders back against the logs. Wiles looked at him a trifle sourly.

"Sure you have," he said. He stood staring at Aige for a minute, during which the storekeeper grinned even more broadly. "All right, what's the joke? And it'd better be funny. We can tuck three people away as easily as two."

"Well, it *is* funny," said Aige. He pointed. "That's Cary Longan."

Wiles glanced at Cary.

"So that's his name," Wiles said. "All right, what about it?"

"Nothing," said Aige. "Just that Cary's got a reputation for keeping his word. Done business with him some years now; and it's true. He always keeps his word."

"What're you babbling about?" snapped Wiles. "What's his word got to do with it?"

"He just gave it. That's what makes it so funny," said Aige. "Here you are making all these plans for what you're going to do with him and Miss Orvalo, and he already told you you're a dead man. Here you are, making plans like mad, and on his word you been dead for three minutes—"

With a sudden movement, Aige jerked the harness spike-punch loose from the log wall beside him and threw it to Cary, ducking back around the corner of the building. Cary caught the tool in midair, threw it in one direction, and dove in the other, rolling head over heels on the ground until his body covered his dropped gunbelt. He came out of his final roll holding his short gun and firing at the three loopers with the energy rifles.

98.

They were already firing back—to where Cary had been a split second before. A bullet from Cary's short gun hit one of them high in the shoulder, so that he seemed to fling his weapon from him. The other two dropped their guns and backed off, hands up.

"Get their rifles, Aige," called Cary, rising to his feet.

He turned toward Wiles. But Mattie was there before him, kneeling beside the man, who was lying on his back, choking out his life with the needle shaft of the harness spike-punch through his throat. Cary turned away and went to squat beside the dark form of Charlie, now no longer quivering. He felt for a heart beat and found it. With a deep sigh, he sat back on his heels and began to explore with gentle fingers the bloody area on the side of Charlie's head, which was now beginning to swell.

He got up to go to the loaded travois and bring back the medical kit. He cleaned the damaged area of blood and began to dress the wound. A shadow fell across it, and he looked up.

It was Mattie.

"He's dead, Cary," Mattie said.

Cary glanced over at Wiles, who now lay still, the punch still in his throat. Cary nodded, and turned back to his work on Charlie.

"He's dead." It was Mattie's voice again, making him look up. Her face stared down at him from only inches away. "Cary, *it's wrong to kill!*"

He stared at her. Then he spoke to her, meaning to sound no different than ever; but his voice changed somehow in his throat and came out with a tone he had never used to her before.

"Mattie," he said, "get out of my light."

All the color went out of her face. She straightened up

and stepped back from him. He bent his head once more over Charlie and went back to the business of bandaging. After he had finished this, he lifted Charlie gently back onto a bed made of two sleeping bags lashed on top of the statue on the travois. It was as he was doing this that Charlie's eyes opened, and the swamp otter stirred.

"All right?" asked Cary. He whistled at Charlie.

Charlie whistled back, at first weakly, and then more strongly. The notes of his last whistles were demanding.

Cary nodded and got to his feet. He turned and looked, but he was alone with the dead body of Wiles. He walked around the front of the building and in through the door on the porch.

The three remaining loopers were not to be seen, but he found Aige by the counter where they had all been grouped earlier. Aige was standing over Mattie, who sat with a coffee cup held in both hands, hunched over it as if it was the only source of heat in an icy world.

"Cary." Aige acknowledged Cary's presence as he came up. "I locked those three up in a storeroom. Miss Orvalo here's some upset."

"Mattie," said Cary softly to her. "Charlie's all right, he says. He doesn't want to waste time. He wants to get going."

She paid no attention to him. She spoke above the coffee cup in a low voice, not to either of them, to no one.

"It was for money I wanted to bring the statue down to the city," she said. "And now a man's dead. Because I wanted money."

Aige looked at Cary. Cary bent over her.

"Mattie!" he said, more loudly.

She did not move for a second. Then she straightened up

slowly, as if her attention had just been caught. She set the cup carefully aside.

"What is it?" she said.

"We've got to be moving on," Cary said.

"Yes," she said, and looked at Aige. "What do we owe you, Mister Apfur?"

"Hundred and forty script," Aige answered. "You don't have to pay now, though. I can put it on the books and the next time Cary's by—"

"Never wait to collect what's owed you, Mister Apfur." Stiffly, she got to her feet and reached into one of the inside pockets of her jacket, bringing out a fold of script. "A hundred and forty, you said?"

"Be back in a minute," said Aige, ducking around her. "While you're counting out there. . . ."

He went out the door to the porch without finishing his sentence. Mattie carefully counted out a hundred and forty dollars in script and laid them on the counter. She turned toward the door.

"Wait," said Cary.

She stopped and stood waiting without asking why. After a few minutes, Aige came back in and held the door open for them.

"I'll see you off," he said. "I suppose you're heading for the Strike, Cary? Ought to make it by sunset with no trouble. Those are prime oxen. If you don't—it's near a full moon. Couple hours travel after moonrise'll see you on the bank of the Strike for sure—"

"Mister Apfur," Mattie interrupted him as they moved off the porch, out of the shadow of its roof into the sunlight, and turned left. "You'll notify the Arcadia City authorities about this?"

"Guess so," said Aige to her. "Ordinarily, we don't say anything—there's no City law up here anyway. But since these loopers belong to the mortgage company, I'd probably better. I'll hand the other three over to the airboat pilot when he comes in tomorrow, along with a report on the whole thing, explaining how they started it. You don't need to worry about how the story'll be told."

"That wasn't my worry, Mister Apfur," said Mattie.

They turned the corner. The travois was there waiting for them, and Charlie lifted his head from the sleeping bags. The body of Wiles had disappeared.

"Well, good luck," said Aige, as Cary took hold of the halter rope of the off ox and began to lead the pair with the travois behind them up the slope behind the store building. "Just turn those cattle loose when you reach the Strike and they'll find their way back to me here in a day or so."

"Right," said Cary, moving off without looking around. "Thanks for all, Aige."

"Welcome!" Aige called after them. They mounted the slope and went down the other side into rolling landscape of thigh-high grass, ranging in color from light brown through gray to black. There were only a few isolated trees to be seen between them and the now cloudless horizon.

They began their crossing of the plains area, moving along together without talking. As the sun rose toward noon, this silence between them became a part of the day, with its sun, its continual small varying breezes that left the footsteps of their passage in the bending grasstops, and an occasional working snort from one of the oxen. At first Charlie also was silent, riding the travois. But after a while he began to talk to himself in small, musical whistlings. Looking back once, Cary saw the swamp otter stretched out on his sleeping bags with his head near the head of the statue as if he was holding a conversation with the dark, tooth-chiseled stone.

To reach the dark, broad waters of the Strike River, it took them the rest of a day's silent journeying, with the native winged orthopters rising from the sea of grass before them and settling to one side or another with small insect sounds. In fact, the early-rising moon was well above the horizon and the sun had been down better than an hour when they at last halted on the river bank in a grove of oak and bire.

The nearly full moon had made travel possible, but it did not throw enough light for proper raft-building. They made camp and turned in early. Cary was up before the first dawn paleness had begun to appear in the sky. Once again he washed and scraped his beard, while coffee water came to a boil on the wick-stove. In her sleeping bag and hammock Mattie still slept; and Charlie too was asleep. He drank coffee and went off into the tree grove with an ax.

By the time the sun was clear of the horizon, he had the logs cut, pulled to the clearing, and ready to tie. Glancing over at Mattie, he saw her eyes open, watching him; but she was still in her sleeping bag.

By the time he had finished tying the raft together with wire, the day was beginning to warm as the sun beat more directly down on them. Mattie, Cary saw, was up now; but she had still made no move to start breakfast. Cary went over and started it himself. By the time the pressed brick of meat and vegetables had softened in the cooking water and turned into a stew, the biscuits and coffee also were ready. Mattie still had not come over to the stove. Cary filled her plate and carried it to her.

"Thanks," she said in a low voice, not looking up as she took plate and eating tools from him.

He stood over her as she took the plate into her lap—sitting cross-legged on the ground at the foot of her hammock—and began to eat.

"Don't want to rush you, Mattie," he said, "but we've no time to burn. Soon's we eat, we better get loaded and started downriver."

At that, she did raise her head. Her face was drawn and her eyes looked bleakly into his.

"I'm not going anywhere today," she said. "It's a Prayer Day."

He stared at her.

"Prayer Day?"

"Haven't you kept count?" she said. "This is the seventh day since we started; and it was a Prayer Day the day I found you and brought you back to my premises. I couldn't start then because it was a Prayer Day; and I'm not going to go on now, on a Prayer Day."

He shook his head, as if to shake her words into some pattern of common sense.

"Mattie—"

"I'm not going to talk about it," she said.

She set down the plate, got to her feet, and walked over to the pile of gear. She rummaged in her personals bag and came out holding the familiar white volume with the writing, fire-red letters. Opening it, she sat down and began to read, there by the gear, ignoring her breakfast which still sat beside the hammock. Cary studied her for a long moment and then turned away.

He went back and ate his own breakfast, then methodically set about striking camp. He packed up his own hammock and the rest of the gear except Mattie's hammock, bag, and the still untouched plate of stew. Then he dug some deep stake holes at the river's edge, planted anchor posts in them, and block-and-tackled the raft to the edge of the water.

He levered it into the shallows at the edge of the bank and began loading it. Still, Mattie had not stirred. She sat, still reading.

Charlie looked curiously from her to Cary as Cary went on about loading the statue and the gear aboard the raft. After a while he whistled curiously at Cary.

Cary whistled back shortly and shook his head. Charlie queried him again, but this time Cary only shook his head. Then Charlie turned and made his own way to the raft, lying down on it beside the head of the statue. The sun by now was several hours up from the horizon, and there was nothing left to pack but Mattie's gear.

Cary walked over to her.

"Mattie," he said. "Charlie and I both got a stake in getting that statue into town on time."

She put a finger in her book to mark her place, closed it, and looked up.

"Charlie and you?" she said. "I know what stake you've got in getting it to town. You're looking forward to mixing in with all that hoorah and celebrating when the mortgage is signed, with your pockets full of money to throw around. But don't tell me Charlie knows who that statue's going to, or what it's worth to you and me to get it there by a certain time."

He looked down at her for a long second.

"Charlie may not know who," he said, "but he knows the statue's going someplace where it'll maybe finally be appreciated. And he knows there's some hurry to get it there. As for what it's worth—what it's worth to me is seeing Charlie knowing somebody understands what he's done, before he dies. Comes to the money being that important, you get aboard the raft now and you can have my share. Sure, I like cash when I'm in town, like anyone else; but I don't got to have it or die, like you City people. Out here, money don't do nothing for anyone. Long as I got my gear, my weapons, and some ammunition, there's not a thing more I need in the upcountry."

She kept her eyes on her book.

"This is a day of rest," she said. "Not a day for the taking or making of profit—which is what I'd be doing if I had anything to do with moving that statue further toward the City today."

He shook his head.

"We got to go," he said. "And we're going, Mattie."

"I'm not," she said, calmly.

"I can't leave you alone out here," he answered. "Have to take you whether you want to go on or not, Mattie."

"You signed a contract with me," she said, clearly and still calmly. "You can't sell that statue to the art dealer if I say no. Put me on that raft by force, and you'll hear 'no' from me for now and ever—if you carry the statue and Charlie to Arcadia City times over."

She stopped speaking. He stood, looking down at her, saying nothing.

"Go if you want," she said. "I won't try to stop you. But I'm staying here."

She opened her book and went back to her reading. For a second more he watched her. Then he turned and went to his own gear. He brought his own long gun back, laid it beside her, and went to the raft.

Charlie whistled. Cary answered. He untied the shore line, stepped aboard the raft, and picked up a pole. He pushed strongly with the end of the pole against the bank,

106.

and the front of the raft swung out into the stream until the current caught it and pulled it slowly from shore.

In a minute, it was floating downriver over a bottom too deep for the pole to work against. Cary pulled the pole inboard, laid it down, and went back to take the rudder oar. Steering the raft into the central current, he looked back up toward the campsite, now steadily falling behind them.

Mattie still sat where he had left her, reading. The brilliant white cover of the book caught the sunlight and seemed to burn in her hands as she held it. She had not changed position, and she did not move as he watched. But as the raft moved away from her, she dwindled steadily in size until she was so small that her seated figure could be covered by the tip of his uplifted little finger. Then the raft swam around a bend in the river, and she was lost to sight.

9.

As the black limbs and the dark green leaves of the trees moved between the raft and the view of Mattie, Charlie whistled sharply. The otter was up on all fours, standing by the statue with neck outstretched toward Cary. As Cary looked at him, Charlie whistled again and looked back toward the river bend questioningly.

Cary shook his head and turned his gaze once more to the water before the raft, settling the shaft of the steering oar under his arm.

Charlie whistled a third time.

"No!" snapped Cary aloud. He shook his head, two sharp, distinct moves from one side to the other. "She wants it like that!"

Charlie stopped whistling. The effort of standing was beginning to show on him. His legs bowed and gave under him so that he sank to the raft. Still he held his head up for a long moment on his slim neck, looking at Cary.

Cary stared stone-eyed as a statue himself at the water ahead.

Charlie's neck bent. His head dropped to the logs beneath it. He whistled once more, almost as if to himself, a low, long-drawn-out whistle that faded into silence at last.

With Cary at the oar, they drifted on downriver in silence.

Cary whistled, abruptly and fiercely, and Charlie's head came up. Cary had shoved the steering oar to one side, and the raft was now drifting slowly at an angle back toward the land. As soon as it grounded close to the right-hand bank, Cary jumped overboard with a rope, hauled the raft as close to the bank as it could be pulled in the gravel shallows, and ran ashore.

He tied the rope hastily to the twisted trunk of a bire tree, and turning, headed through a clump of bushes at a steady lope back upstream alongside the river. He ran lightly and easily, without heavy breathing, but with his mouth in a thin line and his eyes fixed ahead. Twice he was forced to head inland from the river, but always he turned back to the bank at the first opportunity. And it was only a few moments before he came out through the trees where he had cut logs for the raft that morning, and found Mattie still sitting as he had left her, the book in her hands.

He stopped running and walked up to her. She did not look at him as he approached. Her eyes were still on the pages of the book before her. He came up and stood over her.

"Mattie," he said.

She did not answer. Her attention was all on the pages before her. He reached down to take the book from her, and his fingers touched her hands. They were chill to the touch.

His expression changed. He bent and looked into her down-tilted face. It was as white as the face of a woman in shock.

"Mattie—" he said. Gently, he put his fingers under her chin and forced her face up to look at him.

"What're you doing here?" she whispered.

"Guess I can't leave you, Mattie," he said, and let her go, straightening up to look at her almost grimly. "Never thought there was nobody I couldn't leave, nothing I couldn't do. But I can't go on and leave you here. Guess you've done that for me. So we'll stick with you, if you won't move, Charlie and I."

"You're wrong," Mattie said, barely above the level of the whisper in which she had answered first. "This time, you're wrong. You ought to go on. Leave me."

"Like this?" Cary's straight, dark brows came together in a line across his face. "Leaving you with the long gun and a day's walk back to Aige's is one thing. This here's something else. You planning to sit here and die, Mattie?"

There was a sick feeling in him that came out in his voice, and she heard it.

"I don't suicide! You think that of me?" she flared for a second; and then the coldness took the life out of her voice again. "You don't understand."

"What don't I understand?"

"The universe is not mocked," she said, not looking at him, rocking herself a little. "There is a physics of life, and what is taken must be counterbalanced by what is given—"

"Mattie!" The hardness of his voice stopped her voice and her body movement, all at once. "What you talking about?"

"You killed a man," she said. "I was the cause of it, but you were the instrument. A man was killed for the sake of worldly gain." She looked up at him. "It's wrong to kill, Cary. To kill puts you in debt to the natural law of the universe. It makes you vulnerable. You killed him and the law of averages is against you now. I was the cause. If something happens to me, that helps to balance the forces. Oth-

110.

erwise the physics of the universe stays tilted against you. You killed—"

"Mattie!"

The sudden explosion of his voice stopped her, but only briefly.

"You don't understand," she said, dully.

"It's you who don't understand," he answered. "You think you got some reason to pay out for me? There's nothing you owe, Mattie. Me neither. Mister takes a weapon to me, I take one to him—it was him started it, not me."

"But you killed him. There's man dead back there—"

"I killed him because Charlie was laying there like he was dead. I thought he was," Cary said. "Thought the looper'd killed him."

"Even if he had," said Mattie. "It's not the same thing. That looper was a man—"

"Charlie's a man!"

A black, hot tide washed over him for a second, so that he could not see. When he had his sight back, he saw Mattie sitting frozen, staring up at him. The fury in him had finally stopped her mouth.

"You listen to me," he said, barely above a whisper, and the jagged words tore his throat raw, getting out. "Charlie's a man. You know who's not a man? That looper's not a man. None of them's men. No mister on this planet, not Aige, not me—none of us, men—to Charlie's people. And that's what counts."

She leaned back a little from him. He bent down over her.

"You know what we are?" he said, low-voiced. "We're animals. Aliens. We're alien animals come out of someplace else where we had a right to be, to here where we got no right. And you know what we do, now we're here? We poison the earth and kill off the vine and the char. We bring in our own plants that got no right here, neither, and we plant them to drive out the plants that belong here. And you know what else we do? We cut, and we burn, and we build; and finally, we go and kill men and women—real men and women with a right here, because it's their world—in order to skin them and sell their hides to be shipped off the planet to other animals like us who don't even know where those hides came from."

He stopped to draw breath, and the air seemed burned like flame against his raw, tight throat.

"I told you, Mattie," he said. "I told you Charlie's people hadn't any use for me. I told you they didn't think it was any great thing, my keeping the trappers off them. And I guess you thought that was real strange of them. Strange? Strange they don't feel grateful and thankful an alien animal like me don't come around killing their brothers and sisters and wives and children no more? Grateful one like me stops another from killing them? That's some real great kindness and favor, is it then?"

He broke off.

"But Charlie, he's even more than the men the rest of his people are," he said. "Because Charlie can see an alien like me hidden in a dirty chunk of stone and carve that stone until it's art—until that alien's there for all to see. You and I can't do that; but he can."

He turned and strode off blindly. It was only when bire branches whipped him in the face that he realized what he was doing. Then, with a great sweep, the fury left him, and his mind cleared. Suddenly he felt washed clean, empty, and hollow inside. It was not like him, talking so much. He turned around. Mattie was still seated, staring wordlessly after him with a white face. He went back to her. Taking her hand, he pulled her to her feet.

"Sorry, Mattie," he said, more quietly. "Sorry. It's not you—it's a thousand misters like those loopers, over the past six years. Listen—if you're right and the universe makes all even, it don't matter then what shape of body there is about a person. If I'd done nothing back there, it'd be Charlie dead now, and that looper living. Happen it's the looper that's dead and Charlie's still alive. We didn't start what happened, none of us—Charlie, you, or me. It was the loopers figured to kill Charlie and smash his statue from the first, before we even showed up at Aige's. If it's a universe knows what happens, then it's a universe knows that it had to be Charlie or the looper. And the one which lived had the best right to be living."

She shook her head, her face still white, but said nothing.

"Makes no matter now, anyway," Cary said. "Raft's at the bank, just below the bend there, and we aren't going further today. You'll walk that far to be with the rest of us, even if it's a Prayer Day, sure?"

"Yes," she said.

"Good. I'll help strike your hammock here and pack up," said Cary, moving to do just that. In a few minutes he had the gear he'd left with her packed and ready to carry. He took it in a bundle over his right shoulder, and with the long gun in his left hand, he led her back down along the river toward the raft.

When they reached the bushes screening the spot just upstream of where the raft had touched the shore, for the first time Cary became conscious of a sound from just ahead where the raft would be. It was a steady, rhythmic thumping and rustling like nothing he had ever heard before. A small noise, but strange. Dropping the gear, he sprinted ahead of Mattie, into the clearing.

Charlie was no longer on the raft. He was ashore, and the trail of crushed grass in the soft earth of the river bank showed how he had gotten there. His eyes were closed, his jaws were lathered in foam and snapped unceasingly, and his body and limbs jerked and twitched with such force that he moved about on the ground. The sharp odor that had accompanied his earlier violent outburst against his own people when they had left the plateau was heavy in the air.

Cary dropped at the otter's side and tried to hold the jerking body still, but it was too strong for him. He felt himself violently shoved aside. Looking up, he saw Mattie, who knelt in his place beside Charlie.

"Convulsions!" Mattie snapped at him. "Don't you know convulsions when you see them?"

She grabbed up an eight-inch length of stick, perhaps two inches in diameter, from the ground nearby and thrust it between Charlie's mindlessly snapping jaws. The swamp otter's chisel teeth went through the wood as if it were a twig. Mattie reached up blindly, pulled Cary's short gun from its holster, and thrust the gun barrel between Charlie's jaws. The gleaming teeth clicked and chewed on the metal, but could not cut it through. She reached in a finger behind the barrel to pull Charlie's long, black tongue clear of his throat.

"Sleeping bags!" she cried. "Liners. Anything to wrap him in, Cary! We've got to get him warm!"

Cary turned and jumped onto the raft. When he came back a moment later with his arms full of bedding gear, Charlie was still convulsing. Dark blood had begun to trickle from his nostrils, staining purple the lather and foam

114.

just below the nostrils. Together Mattie and Cary wrapped the twitching body thickly in bedding and held the bedding in place with their arms in a cocoon of warmth about Charlie.

Gradually, his convulsions became less violent. They slowed and became intermittent. Finally, they dwindled to heavy shudders and then stopped entirely. Charlie at last lay still, but his eyes were still closed and he breathed heavily through his blood-encrusted nostrils.

Mattie met Cary's eyes and sat back, letting go of the bedding she and Cary had been holding in place about the swamp otter. Cary let go also. Mattie kneeling, Cary squatting, they looked across Charlie at each other.

"Nothing to do now but wait," said Mattie.

They got to their feet. With the automatic motions of habit, Cary set up the wick-stove and made coffee. They sat drinking coffee and saying little while the sun rose to noon overhead and started to lower toward the western horizon beyond the other side of the river.

Charlie still lay, breathing heavily, his eyes closed, when they checked him for perhaps the dozenth time.

"When did he eat last that you know of?" Mattie asked Cary.

"Pool at the foot of the cliff," said Cary. "Unless he was in the water some of the nights while we were sleeping. But I don't guess he was."

"I guess not," said Mattie. She reached out her hand, first over the area of his bandaged shoulder, and then over the swollen side of Charlie's head where the dead looper had struck him. "Feel."

Cary put out his own hand. Over both damaged areas, he could feel the feverish heat radiated up against his palm.

"I don't suppose it'd make any difference, here or on the raft," said Mattie. She glanced at the sun. "You suppose he'd want to move on?"

"Guess so," said Cary.

Mattie got to her feet.

"Then we'd better travel while the light lasts," she said.

10.

Cary looked at her, and she looked away from him. He nodded and got to his feet.

"Sure," he said. "We'll get packed and moving."

He folded up the wick-stove, while Mattie took on board the raft the gear he had left with her and which she had carried in from the bushes after Cary had dropped it there to run to Charlie. Last of all, they carried Charlie gently on a blanket-wrapped litter out to the raft and laid him on a soft pile of bedding beside the statue. He showed no signs of knowing he was being moved. His eyes were still closed, and his breathing sounded heavily. Cary shoved the raft off from the bank once more into the main current of the broad, dark river.

The day had begun bright, with only a few clouds. But during the morning a haze had moved in, and by the time they were once more on their way, the haze had been replaced by a cloud cover that was almost solid from horizon to horizon. Under these clouds, the day itself seemed dulled, and all its sounds muted. They went down the brown flow of water with hardly a gurgle, as Cary moved the steering oar to avoid a floating deadhead or one of the occasional rocks to break the surface of the stream.

The grasslands they had crossed by oxen and travois were being left behind them now. At first only in patches but then more solidly, the forest area began to close in about both sides of the river. The forest here was barely touched by human influence. Here and there a solitary variform oak could be seen with its stiffly upright trunk and limbs stretched out at right angles to the trunk's vertical line. But all around were bire and temp, sourbark, and bushes of poison thorn. They all wound about with the great green hawsers of midland vine and the heavy dull-purple bunches of the epiphytic char, that was both blossom and fruit at once, clinging with invisible root filaments to the rest of the vegetation on which it parasitically fed.

As the sky darkened overhead with the clouds and the lowering sun, so the forest darkened, closing in around the river on which they traveled. By nearly sunset, shadow and dark color—the black and gray and deep brown of the trees and the dusky purple of the char—surrounded them on every side. The woods were strangely quiet after the insect-filled plains—only an occasional hooting or whistling came from their depths.

"The loopers wouldn't like it here," said Mattie, unexpectedly.

Cary looked about him. It was true. Everyone knew that loopers found Arcadia a drab, dark world compared to whatever they had been accustomed to on other planets where men had settled. Mostly, on Arcadia, people born here figured that the loopers' reaction was just another way of looking down their noses at a new world struggling to pay off its first mortgage. But, watching the surrounding forest now, Cary suddenly understood something of how the loopers must feel.

118.

It must look chill-like to them, he thought, something like this river and forest—chill-like, sad-making, even fearful—a fearful, sorrowful sort of place, with its duns and grays and blacks and heavy purples.

"You're likely right," he said to Mattie.

Just as he spoke, the sun—low on the horizon now, down behind the nearer treetops—broke through the clouds just before setting. Suddenly the forest was flooded by a back-lighting of fiery illumination that sought through the upper branches of the twisted bire and the other trees, making their limbs stand out twisted and black and stark. Not just a fearful, sorrowful place now—but such a place, hell-lighted, it would seem to loopers. But to Cary and Mattie, watching, it was sweet and beautiful.

The land, the trees, the vine, the char, and the river—all of them—were tied together into something to touch you, deep inside, by the last light of the day. It was a hard, dark land, this Arcadia, but there was something strong in it to make you love it, like a song heard far off and going away just as the sun goes down, once you were born to this world and grown up on it.

They ran on through the forested country under a bright moon until midnight, with Cary at the steering oar. At midnight Mattie relieved him. He barely had time to pull a sleeping bag liner over him before he fell into slumber.

He woke to find it nearly day, rolled himself up into a sitting position at the side of the raft, and splashed cold water on his face. Awake, he went back to Mattie.

"Your turn," he said. "I'll take the oar now."

She nodded wearily, gave him the oar, and went forward to drop down on the bedding he had just abandoned, pulling sleeping bags and liners into a mound over her.

119.

Cary settled himself to his steering. Reaching overside with one hand, he brought up a palmful of cold water and drank. The river current was steady now, and they were making good time.

During the next few hours, however, the river widened and slowed. It was now perhaps twice as wide from bank to bank as it had been up in the forest, and occasionally they drifted past a log hutch with a woven vine roof blackened by the sun, perched on the very edge of the water. But there was no sign of life to be seen about any of these buildings.

"Voting," said Cary to himself, looking at the tenth one they had passed since his wakening. "Gone to the City, likely." He glanced at the mound of bedding that was Mattie, but it gave no sign of anyone awake within it. He weighed the idea of tying up the raft to the bank and resting now, against the hope of finding a chance to rest later. But the City was still distant, overland; and with Charlie the way he was . . . sleep later was the word. Himself, he could always make do one way or another.

He steered on into the rising brilliance of morning that was making the river now into a white ribbon of light.

After a while, when the sun stood at about ten o'clock, he steered the raft to the bank and stepped ashore to set up the wick-stove and make some coffee. When it was ready, he filled a cup and carried it onto the raft. Cup in hand, he squatted beside the pile of bedding hiding Mattie and carefully lifted back sleeping bag liners until he uncovered her face.

For a moment he squatted there, cup in hand, looking at her. In the bright midmorning light, her sleeping face was wiped smooth of most of the tightness that it held always when he had seen her back in the City and oftentimes during waking hours on this trip with the statue. Interestingly, he found himself remembering what she had said, the day before they had left, when she had asked him how old he was. How old had she said she was?

Nineteen. Usually, she looked older. Well, not older, but some general age between nineteen and middle age. Now though, sleeping, she looked younger. Cary tried to remember what his younger sister had looked like before she died of a bad cold. Mira had been—what was it? Twelve. She had been the last of the family to die. Cary wondered—if Mira had lived would he have stayed in the City like Mattie?

Probably not. Mira would have turned woman and got married or got a job or something. Anyway, he had wanted to go to the upcountry, even then. He had tried to talk his dad into it. . . . His thoughts came back from their wandering. What was it he had had in mind? Oh, yes—Mira, when she was young and sleeping. Was that what Mattie looked like now?

He considered Mattie's slumbering face, thoughtfully, the cup of coffee growing cool in his hand. No, there was something there like Mira, but it was different. They were all different, just the way no two swamp otters were alike. Charlie was one in a million. Mattie too. Strange where they came from, different from all the rest. Strange where they went to. But Mattie was no otter; she was a woman. . . .

Mattie's eyes slowly opened, then blinked against the light of the sun. She turned and hid her face in the bag liner beneath her.

"What is it?" she asked, muffledly.

"Brought you some coffee," said Cary. He became aware of the temperature of the cup in his hand. "Better warm it though. Stay put."

He went back to the fire, poured the cold cup back into the pot, swished it around with the warm coffee, and filled the cup again and brought this to Mattie. She was up on one elbow under the covers when he brought the cup of fresh coffee. She smiled when she took it from him.

"Thank you kindly, Cary," she said. She sipped at it. "Tastes good."

He stayed squatting, watching her drink it. She became aware of his gaze on her and looked down at the cup.

"Where are we?" she asked. "What's going to happen today?"

He heard her, but he paid her words almost no attention. "Mattie. . . ." he began.

Her head lowered further toward the coffee. The line of her mouth grew hard.

"You didn't answer me," she said, sharply, but not looking up. "I said—"

"Hush, Mattie," he said gently. "I've something to talk to you about—"

She sat up suddenly, spilling coffee on the sleeping bag liners. Her face was tight again.

"No!" she said. "I don't want to talk. I've got no time for talk. It's no use talking to me, anyway. Money's all I'm interested in—money's all I'm ever going to be interested in. I learned that the hard way, trying to stay alive, and it's too late to unlearn it now. I'm what I am, and I wouldn't change if I could. So, there's no point my talking to anybody about anything else. Not to you—not to anybody!"

Abruptly, she scrambled to her feet and stood looking around her.

"We're tied up," she said. "Why? Why aren't we moving? You realize we've only got three days to get to the City in time to meet that art buyer of yours?"

Slowly, Cary uncoiled to his own upright height. He looked down at her a little sadly.

"Time to eat a bite, Mattie," he said. "Come ashore and we'll cook something."

11.

They made a late breakfast on the bank over the wick-stove, and then reboarded the raft and put it out into the current again.

"Lock and dam not too far down from here," said Cary to her. "Once past that, it's only a few klicks until we've need to leave the river and begin travel overland to town. Happen we can pick up oxen and a wagon from there on into town."

"How far from here to the City?" Mattie asked.

"Three days, not more," said Cary. "We ought to be there just in time—for voting and for Mister Waters, that's the art buyer."

Mattie nodded.

"Good," she said. She was fussing over Charlie, cleaning him up, in fact.

"Fever's down a little more, it seems," she said. "I wish he'd come to, though. Cary, do they usually stay unconscious this long when they've been hurt?"

Cary shook his head.

"Never seen it," he answered. "I told you, I don't know that much about them. I can talk a little with Charlie, and there was that time in the beginning I lived a while where they have all their hutches—or nests, or mudball dens, whatever you call them. I've helped some when one'd get shot or trapped. But there's little I really know about them any more than the next mister."

"But there ought to be something we can do!"

Cary looked down at his boots and shook his head emptily.

"Wait," he said. "That's all."

A little later they came around a very wide, sweeping curve of the river into what was almost a small lake of its ponded waters. At the far end a dam and buildings of white concrete glittered against the dark land—almost eye-hurting in their reflection of the sunlight. An opened spillway in the right part of the dam beside the lock let dark water through.

Cary angled the raft to a landing on the side of the lake near the lock. A slight figure with a soft brown beard, wearing woodsman clothes and carrying the inevitable long gun, wandered down to the shore of the open grassy area where they landed. He stepped knee deep into the water and helped pull the raft into shore, to tie up.

"Thank you, mister," said Cary to him, when the raft was at last tied and they were all, except Charlie, standing on the bank.

"My pleasure, mister," answered the small woodsman. He was perhaps a few years older than Cary, but already his face had gone into placid, leathery lines from sun and weather. "I'm Mul Oczorny. You'll be Mister Cary Longan and this"—he turned toward Mattie—"Miss Orvalo?"

"The same," Cary said. He looked at the little man curiously. "We know you, mister?"

Mul shook his head.

"Piece of news about you been broadcast out from the

125.

City," Mul said. "Some looper run into you upcountry, said you were bringing down a statue some sooger of a swamp otter made." He nodded to the raft. "That it? I'd mighty like to take a look."

Cary nodded.

"Statue's for looking. That's why Charlie made it," he said. "Charlie's the name of the otter. You see him there."

"Do," agreed Mul. "Thank you kindly."

He stepped down the bank and lightly onto the raft. He approached the statue and leaned over to inspect it. For more than a few seconds he stood, bent above it, examining the stone shape. Then he straightened up and his eyes went to Charlie, lying beside it.

"This sooger's hurt some," he said.

"Looper gave that news you heard, burned him with an energy rifle," said Cary. "Another looper later on hit him with a sledge."

Mul nodded, looking down at Charlie's still form. Then he turned and came back off the raft up onto the bank to face Cary and Mattie once more.

"Loopers," he said, without emphasis. He turned his head politely to one side and spat green. His brown beard in front was tinged with the color of the fresh-cut vine he had been chewing. He looked back at Cary and Mattie. "That's a mighty fine statue he made there. You, isn't it, mister? Like you was in the stone. I never seen anything so fine and real as that. Guess I understand why you want to get it to the City."

"Karl Turnbull home?" asked Cary, looking across the length of the dam at the white concrete buildings on the far side which housed the electric generating plant powered by the dam structure, and the family that owned and operated the plant.

126.

"Him and his boys. All," said Mul, leaning on his rifle and watching Cary.

"Guess I'll walk over and ask him to let us through the lock," said Cary. He glanced at Mattie. "Supposed to be free—passage through that lock. But it's a kindly thing offering to pay him something. You mind paying?"

"If that's what's done, all right," said Mattie.

Cary nodded. He picked up his own rifle and walked away from Mattie and Mul, down to the near end of the dam. He stepped up on it and began to cross it. A catwalk ran the full length of the structure, suspended airily on a pair of stressed concrete girders over the open spillway. Cary strolled on over and up to the door in the largest concrete building on the dam's far side. He knocked.

"Come in," said a voice from within.

Cary laid his hand on the door panel and pushed it open. He stepped into a small room like an office, fitted with a pair of heavy wooden desks and several sets of plyboard files. The back of the room was closed off by a wall-sized sliding panel from the rest of the interior of the building. Behind the farthest of the desks sat a heavy man in his forties with coal-black hair and eyebrows.

"Mister Turnbull," Cary nodded at him. "Likely you don't remember me? I'm Cary Longan, from upcountry."

"Remember you," said Turnbull. He was clad in upcountry pants and woven shirt, but his skin was almost as pale as the skin of someone from Arcadia City. "I know all about you. Heard about you and that outfitter miss and the statue and otter on the broadcast from the City."

"Honored," said Cary. "Then I guess you can figure what I'm here for. We'd take it kindly if you'd open the gates to your lock and lock us down to the lower river below your dam."

Turnbull leaned forward. Both his arms lay on the desk already; and as he hunched over them, the muscles in the big forearms swelled and his fists closed.

"I'll see you all dead, first, Longan!" he said. "You think my great-grandfolks worked their heads off back before emigration so they could bring in enough funds to buy a power station out of the first mortgage here on Arcadia— and for four generations we've built on and saved cash here for the day when the second mortgage'd be signed and peo-ple'n industry'd move upcountry—you think we went through that for five generations, and I'm going to help you move that chunk of rock down to the City to bust up all chance for a second mortgage? You must be full of bad weed, woodie!"

Cary did not move. But his voice became quieter and his eyes more alert to watch the office about them.

"You're not making much sense, mister," he said. "We're just taking a statue down to sell it to a looper art buyer from the Old Worlds."

"Statue!" Turnbull jumped to his feet and came around the desk. He was not short. But he was shorter than Cary, so that his bulk made him look abnormally broad, like the lower half of a dutch door. He stamped across the room to the wall beside the door where Cary had come in. There was a scope-screen there, with controls below it. Turnbull punched buttons and the meter-wide screen lit up with a view of the raft across the ponded water behind the dam. They saw the raft, what was on it, and both Mattie and Mul beyond as if from a distance of less than that of the raft's length itself.

"Look at that!" Turnbull grunted. "If it was a real statue, I might believe there was something sensible to it—

128.

not just that crazy upcountry hate you woodies have for anything that looks like decent, high-class civilization. But that's no statue—look at it! A chunk of old rock with a few grooves in it, that's all that is—"

"It's a statue, mister," said Cary softly.

"Don't try telling me that! It's part of this crazy deal all you upcountry people have for this world the way it is. Who cares what a world is to begin with? The point is, it ought to end up civilized, with all the trash weeds and the trash animals and such cleared out and good mutated Earth stock moved in. Good cities. Good, well automated farmland. Neat hunting preserves. Industry. Some good tourist attractions. God knows that's one hell of a lot to hope for on a dingy, dark, dirty, backwoods planet like this one— but my family's invested five generations in just that. And you expect me to help you wreck the chance?"

He turned around, went back to his desk, and sat down.

"Get that rock and that bundle of logs off my lake," he said.

Cary stood for a second, without answering. The silence stretched out in the office and a little bead of sweat ran down the side of Turnbull's angry face.

"Mister," said Cary, finally, quietly, "what set you so much against us?"

"You buying me one?" snorted Turnbull. "This is a power station. We get all the broadcasts from the City. One of the mortgage company surveyors flew down from upcountry nearly a week ago telling how you were bringing that rock in to try and stir up the woodies, and maybe even the farmers against voting in the new mortgage. Told how you jumped him and held guns on him and threatened him. Sure, and the word came how you killed another mortgage company man for just touching the statue, up at Aige Apfur's station. You got nothing to tell me I don't know about you, Longan."

"Just otherways, mister," said Cary slowly. "Doesn't sound to me like you got anything about me or the statue right yet. But I can see there's no use my trying to change your mind. So we won't talk. Just you open up that lock, though—"

Turnbull's hand flicked out and threw a toggle switch on the surface of his desk. Behind him the sliding wall slammed abruptly back into its recess. Revealed behind it were four short young men, each with a rifle at his shoulder aimed at Cary.

"My boys," said Turnbull. "All of them good shots, even if they aren't woodies. You back up slowly now, Longan—back up until you hit the wall and then feel along it to your right for the door button. When you find it, out you go —and no reaching for that short gun at your waist."

Cary looked from the four young men to Turnbull. The family resemblance was plain on all of them. He backed away as Turnbull had said, felt along the wall until his finger touched the smooth, half-round shape of a door button, and pressed it. The door opened behind him, and he backed out.

"Be gone by morning," said Turnbull. "One way or another—I don't care which. But be gone by morning or me and the boys'll open fire on you from the top of the generator building."

The door closed in Cary's face. He stood for a moment, gazing at its blank surface of pressed concrete, like the heavy concrete walls of the building surrounding it. Then he turned and headed back across the catwalk over the dam.

130.

He found Mul and Mattie seated on the bank with the wick-stove and a coffeepot going between them. Mattie offered him a cup as he came up and he took it without a word.

"Likely," said Mul, looking up at him, "he wasn't friendly, that Turnbull mister?"

Mattie looked startledly at the little man and then back at Cary. But Cary was looking at Mul himself.

"Might have told us," Cary said.

"Thought you'd figure. 'Scuse," said Mul, apologetically. "I said you'd been talked about on the video broadcasts. Figured you'd know he knew."

"He knows wrong," said Cary.

"Cary!" Mattie broke in on him. "What is all this?"

He turned to her.

"That looper that shot Charlie—you remember, back at the foot of the cliff," he said. "Seems the same looper believed what you said, Mattie, about the statue being important. He went on into town and said we were hauling in Charlie's statue to make trouble for those wanting the mortgage voted in. Turnbull, over there, said the statue was supposed to stand for leaving Arcadia the way we want it, us in the upcountry. And we're taking it to the City so woodies and farmers'll see it and not vote for the mortgage."

He stopped and drank from his coffee cup.

"Turnbull's not going to open his lock for us," Cary said. "Raft can't be run over the spillway—it'd break to pieces falling that far to the lower level. But Turnbull's got four sons and rifles. Says for us to clear out by morning, one way or another."

Mul looked across at the heavy concrete building with its parapet roof and high, narrow windows.

131.

"No way to go in and change his mind," Mul said. He looked back at Cary.. "You say he knows wrong?"

"Taking this statue to the City to sell it to a looper art buyer," said Cary.

Mul gazed at him strangely, holding the coffee cup in his hand as if he had forgotten it was there.

"You saying," said Mul slowly, "there's nothing to it?"

"Of course, something's to it!" Cary's voice came as close to sounding his anger as it ever had in his life. "There's something to it for you, for me, for Charlie, even if not for—" he checked himself, catching Mattie's eye, "Turnbull and misters like him."

"But," said Mul, "you're selling it off Arcadia—"

"That's as will be." Cary looked at the smaller man coldly. "It's somehow a business of yours, mister?"

Mul looked back at him simply. Then he put his cup down carefully on the ground of the bank and began to fumble inside his shirt.

"You're Cary Longan," Mul said. "Heard about you more than some little. This hears different from what I heard. Word said what the broadcasts said—you taking a statue to town. No business of mine—you're right. Happen it's something to do with cash, though. I got me some script here—"

He produced a small leather money pouch at the end of a thong around his neck.

"Put it away!" snapped Mattie.

He turned his head slowly to look at her in astonishment, the pouch still held in his hand.

"Put it away, I said!" cried Mattie again. "Do you hear me?"

"Yes, miss," said Mul. He put the pouch back in his shirt. "No offense meant—"

132.

Mattie whirled and stalked off.

"No offense taken," said Cary gently. "It's us ought to be apologizing to you, Mul. Thank you kindly for what you figured to offer."

Mul shrugged embarrassedly and looked at the ground.

"Only script," he said. He cleared his throat and looked up again. "How you going to get the raft and all down below the dam?"

Cary turned his head to look at the woods sloping steeply off at the right end of the dam.

"There a portage around and down?" Cary asked.

Mul nodded.

"Regular trail," he said. "Not wide enough for a raft though, even you've got some way of carrying it."

"Maybe we'll break the raft up, portage the rest, and build a new one out of the timber below."

"No timber there now." Mul shook his head. "Turnbull and his boys logged it off last year. Oh, there's trees, but not for raft-making." He hesitated. "Maybe I could help a small some?"

Cary looked at him closely.

"If I had another man," Cary said, "we could take the raft apart and portage the logs one at a time, maybe. Can't do it alone."

"Miss Orvalo, she can't help either, sure," said Mul. "Too heavy for a woman. I'd be in favor of giving you a hand with those logs myself, you don't mind."

"Don't mind. Thank you kindly," said Cary. "I hoped you'd say something such." He looked at the sun, which was now approaching the noon zenith. "Guess we might get started right now."

Cary had Mul take him down the trail. It was not bad for a portage trail, a little steep in spots, but wide enough to maneuver the logs down it and free of roots and brush underfoot that could trip up whoever was carrying a load down it.

"How about Charlie?" Cary asked Mattie, when the two men got back up to the raft. "Think he's all right to go down on a litter?"

"I think he's better," Mattie said. They were all standing on the raft looking down at the still, black form of the swamp otter. "He's still unconscious, but I've been giving him water and he's been taking it—look."

She reached over the side of the raft, dipped up a cupful of the fresh water, and stepped over to Charlie. Lifting the long upper lip on the top side of his jaw, she poured the water between his long teeth. It disappeared, and they could see the smooth movement of his throat under the black fur of his neck as the swallowing reflex occurred.

"And he doesn't feel so hot now," said Mattie, moving her hand over Charlie's head and shoulder. "Maybe he just needed rest to start to mend." She looked up at Cary. "If you don't joggle him, carrying him down. . . ."

"We'll go sure careful, miss," said Mul.

They carried Charlie down and left him on the litter under the shade of the single large tree that grew among the brush and new growth on the bank of the foot of the dam. Then they returned, to rope and skid the statue down the slope.

During the rest of the afternoon, Mattie carried the smaller pieces of gear down, load by load, while Cary and Mul unwired the logs of the raft and, one by one, struggled with them down the twisting, sloping portage trail.

With practice, they grew experienced and clever. Stripped to the waist, and their lean bodies dripping with sweat under the leather pads strapped to the shoulder on which they each rested an end of the log they were carrying, they learned each hard spot and how it might be avoided or circumvented. There were points where it was necessary to back up to go around a corner. Turns so steep the man behind was well advised to go to his knees to keep from throwing too much of the log's weight on the man at the front. There were slippery spots where the earth had worn slick, protruding tree roots or bushes that could trip feet not expecting them. And, in the end, there was the need to always be braced for a slip or stumble by the man on the other end of the log that might throw unexpected weight upon his partner.

Still, they got the logs down. At first at a steady rate, and then more slowly, as the climb back up the portage trail became steadily more of a trial for already weary legs.

About sunset, with a little less than half the logs yet to go, Cary's feet went out from under him suddenly on a turn. He had sufficiently alert reflexes still to shout a warning to Mul, who was carrying the rear end of the log, and to throw the front end from him as he fell, so that it should not come down on top of him. But, the next thing he knew, both Mul and Mattie—who should have been down at the foot of the portage trail—were bending over him.

"He's got to have some sleep!" Mattie was saying, furiously. "He didn't rest hardly at all last night and not at all yesterday. . . ."

"All right," said Cary, and he struggled to his feet with their hands helping him. But when he was upright, his knees gave like hinges of oiled leather. Although he objected, they led him down to the foot of the portage.

That was the last he remembered, until he woke to new moonlight and sat up to see the outlines of Mul and Mattie seated before a fire.

"What time is it?" he asked. But his glance at the moon and the night shadows had already told him it must be nearly midnight. "Mul, we've need to get those other logs down here before dawn."

The other two, however, insisted he eat first before going back to work. He started to protest, then realized the sense of it. Gratefully, he filled up on hot coffee and canned stew. When it was eaten, Mul offered him a fresh-cut length of vine.

He started to reach for it, glanced at Mattie, and then shook his head.

"Thanks kindly, no," he said.

"Go ahead," said Mattie, roughly.

"No, I guess not," he said slowly. He ran a hand over his chin and found the stubble stiff upon it. He smiled over at Mattie. "Never could go back, once I made up my mind to something. Guess maybe I won't shave, though. Reason in all things."

He got to his feet and, with Mul, headed back up the portage trail through the black shadows and silver light. With the rest and the meal, he felt like a giant. He was almost lightheaded with the strength he had recaptured.

"Doesn't take much to bring a man back," he said to Mul.

"Bear us a few logs down the hill first," remarked Mul. "Then you tell me that."

Nonetheless, although the little man was right and Cary soon found that he had gained back only part of his normally rested energy and power, he was once more up to the work. It was slow; but as dawn was breaking, they brought down the final log, assembled the logs on the bank of the river below the dam, and set about tying them together.

Mattie had fallen asleep by the fire. They let her rest

while they finished tying the raft, and they did not even disturb her when they went over to the wick-stove to make coffee. But, as the water bubbled in the pot, some ancient instinct seemed to rouse her and she sat up, rubbing her eyes.

"All done?" she asked joyously, seeing the assembled raft by the water's edge. She got to her feet. "Here, let me make you something to eat—"

She broke off, turning toward the shadows where Charlie lay.

"I better tend to Charlie first though," she said. "He hasn't had any water since the middle of the night—"

"Just a minute, Mattie," Mul said.

"What?" she turned to him.

"You don't need to water him none," said Mul. He looked down at his coffee cup for a second and then looked up again at both of them. "I checked up on him just a little while after you fell asleep, Mattie, and while you were down with the log we'd just brought, Cary. I didn't see it'd change nothing to speak of it then, rather'n later, so I just let it go until one of you brought it up. The poor sooger's dead. Been dead since just before sunrise."

12.

"*And so we commend him,*" read Mattie, and paused to turn a page in the white book with the fiery red letters on its cover. She searched a moment for the proper commendation, of which there were several at that point in the service. Cary and Mul stood quietly listening and waiting at the side of the newly dug ground; Mattie herself stood at the foot. At the top were a pair of stakes holding a roughed out piece of plank with a message burned into it—the letters having been traced out in vine sap and gunpowder and then set on fire.

CHARLiE
Do not disturb—Cary Longan

". . . *We commend him,*" went on Mattie, having found her place, "*to the universe to which he returns. and from which he will once again return some day, as all things turn and return in time. As the rain to the earth, the water to the stream, the stream to the river, the river to the ocean, and the ocean to the clouds which will fall again in rain, so he to the universe and the universe to him—in that cycle which is without end, unbroken, indestructible, and eternal.*

138.

"Therefore in this way do we find comfort, that our brother Charlie is in no way gone from us, but for the moment passed behind a veil which our temporal and momentary eyes have not the skill to pierce. He is among us yet in all things, though we see him not. He is with us, as we are and shall be with him, now and forever, undeniably."

Mattie closed the book and stopped speaking. They all stood for a second, looking at the mounded earth and the sign; then Mattie turned away and Cary, with Mul, imitated her. They walked slowly back to the raft which was now afloat, tethered to the bank and loaded with all their gear. Cary and Mattie stepped aboard.

"Mul," said Mattie, turning to the smaller man on the bank, "thanks for everything."

"Pleasured myself entirely. No need for thanks," said Mul. He stared earnestly at her. "Likely you've no need for more company, so I'll say my so long here."

Cary turned around.

"You'd care to travel on a ways with us?" he asked.

"Grateful—if not unwelcome."

Cary looked at Mattie.

"Of course, come along!" she said. "What made you think we wouldn't want you after all the help you gave us?"

"Fine statue like that here, you'll not be lacking help," said Mul, stepping onto the raft and jerking loose the tie rope that had held it to the bank. "Thanks kindly though."

They moved out, staying close to the bank until they were well past being level with the spot where the water thundered down from the spillway into the pool at the dam's foot. Then they moved out into midstream of the broadening river where the current now ran more slowly.

"Couple hours we'll be into the farmlands around Beta

139.

Center Grain Elevators," said Cary. "We'll stop off by some likely farm and ask to buy or rent wagon and oxen. Overland then, we ought to be coming into the City by tomorrow morning."

"Will these farmers have phones?" Mattie asked.

"Why, I guess most likely," Cary looked at her. "Bound to be a broadcast unit at Beta Center. Phones'd be cheap to run, with a unit that close."

"They've some little money for such extras too, farmers have," put in Mul.

Mattie nodded. They floated on downriver. Well before noon, they found themselves surrounded on all sides by tilled fields, interspersed with occasional farmhouses, stretching to the horizon in all directions. Occasionally a woman in a yard, a man working in a field, or a child on the river bank, exchanged waves with them.

"There's a possible-looking farm place," said Cary, after a while. He put the steering oar over and shortly they drifted up to a sturdy, dark-wood dock below a farmyard green with variform Earth grass. This was in front of a two-story building of rammed earth blocks patched with narrow, green lowland vines. Beyond the building oxen milled in a corral with a concrete fence.

By the time they had tied the raft to the dock, there were a couple of children down to meet them, a boy about twelve and a girl perhaps half that age. Just behind them came a tall, wide-shouldered woman in her twenties, with a calm face. She was wearing a heavy apron and blacksmithing gloves, which she stripped off to shake hands with Mattie.

"I was shoeing one of the beasts," she said. "Miss Orvalo? I'm Miz Pferden. Saw you coming and phoned my

140.

husband back from the neighbor's. Be here directly." She nodded at Cary and Mul. "One of you're Mister Longan I've no doubt. Broadcasts didn't mention any other."

"Mul Oczorny, Miz Pferden," said Mul. "This mister's Cary Longan."

"It's pleasure to have you as our guests," Miz Pferden said. Her glance went down to the raft. "That the statue? Mind if I look up close at it?"

"Go right ahead, Miz Pferden," Mattie said. "Meanwhile, could I use your phone for a call to the city? I'll find out the charges—"

"Pay no attention to the charges," Miz Pferden said. "We're not a poor family. Been on this land three generations. Stand to get rich from it, selling it for expansion building if the new mortgage gets voted in. But there's no lacking here for us, regardless, even if all mortgages went up in smoke. Svart Pferden'll be with you in a moment— excuse me while I look over that statue."

She went on down to the dock and Mattie went up to vanish inside the house. A few minutes later a light wagon drawn by a single trotting ox came around the house and halted in the graveled road part of the farmyard. A bunchy-shouldered, tough-looking, middle-aged man, an inch or so shorter than the farmwife, got down from the wagon and came up to Cary and Mul.

"Svart Pferden," he said, acknowledging their introductions. "That the statue down there? Excuse me, got to take a look at that."

He went down to join his wife on the dock.

Cary started to follow him, but just then he saw Mattie emerging from the house. She came toward him, walking slowly.

"Something, Mattie?" he asked, as she came up. She raised her face to him, frowning and angry.

"Cary, you must know some hop-skip-and-jump airboat outfit that'll lease to anybody for anything?" she said. "I've called every outfit in town I know and they all pretend they haven't got a free boat to rent us to bring the statue in. It's all because of that story the looper spread about the statue being a symbol of not voting for the new mortgage. People I've lived and dealt with most of my life, and they—"

She broke off.

"Anyway, you must know someone with an airboat who'll rent to us, Cary," she said. "Just tell me who, and I'll get him on the phone."

He gazed at her, troubled.

"Mattie," he said, "thought you didn't want to spend for an airboat. That's why we brought it by hand this far."

"I didn't," she retorted. "But I've changed my mind. Besides, from here on in it won't cost much. Even if it did, I'm not so sure I want to put all my money into subsidiary companies from the new mortgage anyway."

"But that's what you said you've been saving for—all the years I've known you," he said. "You haven't changed mind in just these couple weeks, sure?"

"Maybe I have," she said. "If I have, it's my business, isn't it?"

He nodded slowly.

"Your business," he said slowly. "But it makes some difference to me to know why you'd change."

"You know why!" She flashed an angry glance at him. "Charlie. The loopers. Everything. You're right; all that mortgaging and remortgaging is going to end up doing is leave us one more carbon copy of every other quick-built industrial world. When we aren't—we're Arcadians, with

142.

water and air and land and people like none of the rest of them, and we ought to stay that way!"

The emotional explosion burned itself out suddenly. She stood looking up at him.

"I take it," Cary said, "you won't be voting for the new mortgage yourself?"

She shook her head. He breathed out unhappily.

"Mattie," he said, "I can't let you spend for an airboat, even if you figure you want to now. Happens I lied some to you, after all, about that art buyer."

Her eyes slowly widened, as she stared at him.

"The art buyer," she said. "He—there isn't any art buyer?"

"There's one, right enough," said Cary slowly. "He'll be there too, waiting for us in the City as I said—if he keeps his word. Likewise, he said he'd buy the statue and told me two thousand interworld units. Only one hitch. It wasn't just all that cut and dried. That much money was the most he said he could pay for something like the statue—and only if it turned out he liked it that much."

He stopped talking. Her eyes were still wide open upon him.

"But he'll pay something?" she said.

Cary slowly shook his head.

"Can't be sure, even of that," he said. "He wouldn't pay anything for the little carvings Charlie made. Didn't want them. That's how come I still had them when you hunted me up next morning."

He stopped again. Still, she stood looking at him. They were like two statues themselves when Mul, Miz Pferden, and Svart Pferden himself, with Svart in the lead, broke the spell that bonded the two of them.

"That," said Svart to Cary, coming up from the dock

with his wife and Mul a little behind, "is something I've lived this life to see, that statue. Don't know art—can't make it out all that good, except that it's clear and plainly a statue of you, Mister Longan—but I look at that, and I can feel the earth."

He held out his blunt-fingered, wide-palmed hand, the fingers half-curved upward, in front of Cary.

"I feel the earth, right there. My earth," he said. "Mul here tells me you need wagon and oxen to cart it to the City. I'd be proud, Mister Longan, to drive it myself. And my wife also." He looked at his wife, who nodded.

"Mister Pferden's oxen," she said, "will pull all day and night and never slack until you set your statue down where in the City you wish it. You won't find better carrying by anyone."

Cary looked from her to her husband.

"We were figuring just to rent . . . or buy," he said.

"Rent or buy? Not from me," said Pferden. "I'll carry that statue to town for the pride of it and nothing else, or I'll thank you to ask elsewhere for cartage."

"Mister Pferden," said his wife, placidly, "is a strong-minded man." She looked at her husband, and for a second he looked back at her in a glance of something almost more solid than affection.

Cary nodded.

"If it's that way," he said, "we'd be proud ourselves to have you do so."

"Then it's settled!" said Pferden, almost fiercely. "Got a heavy wagon with a winch and crane already in it. Lend me a hand, misters, and we'll have it out here and the statue in it before a quarter hour's past. Amathea," he turned to his wife, "maybe you and Miss Orvalo would make us up some lunch to take along."

It was closer to an hour, however, before they were actually on their way down the compacted dirt road leading from the Pferden farm toward Beta Center and the direct route to Arcadia City. By that time a small crowd of other farmers had gathered, and with them three woodsmen who said they had been heading to the City from upcountry for Voting Day. They said little; but when the wagon finally started out, they ended up walking along with it, talking in brief, quiet sentences from time to time with Mul, who rode in the rear of the wagon and told them, bit by bit, of his own experiences with the statue and its three escorts.

All along the road to Beta Center, they passed farms where people had come out to the road to speak to them, and sometimes to come close and peer over the wagon sides at the statue. Only one farm produced a tall, round-faced man with a young-looking body but graying hair, who stood squarely in their road.

"Move, Tom," said Svart Pferden from the wagon seat, without raising his voice as the oxen bore down on this man. "I'll drive over you, otherwise."

"You're everybody's fool, Svart!" shouted the man, shaking a finger at Pferden. "Who sold you a license to take the bread we've worked for out of all our mouths, father to son, since folks first landed here?"

But the oxen came close, and he moved aside. Still, his voice shouted after them.

"I'm not the only one sees sense!" he called. "You'll find that out before you're halfway to the City!"

A few moments later a tall young man, panting heavily, burst out of a field of tall grain and fell into step beside the cart. Pferden looked over at him.

"Your dad's not going to be happy with you, Jay," he said.

145.

"Someday—he will—" said the young man, between pants. "You need to understand, Svart. All his life he figured it to come in his time, the second mortgage, and the family'd always remember that. '*It was in Tom Arrens's time we got rich, they'll say,*' he used to tell us. But it's not really the money, it's the happening in his time he wants. Just, he doesn't see yet this *is* the happening, this statue. Later, someday, he'll see."

"Well," Pferden said, flicking the reins to urge the oxen on, "you ought to know your own dad. Like he said, though, there's others feel like him—and for most of them it'll be the money that matters."

They drove on, passing through Beta Center, where several more woodsmen on their way to the City fell in about the wagon. Large numbers, it seemed, not only of the woodies, but of the farmers themselves, were on their way in for the voting, tomorrow. As the afternoon wore on and the sun went westward over the fields of dun-colored grain, less than a week or so from being harvest-ready, the number of those accompanying the wagon with the statue increased. Easily the greatest number of these were woodies —and even now and again one of them would lounge up to the wagon and speak; and Cary would look down from the wagon seat where he sat with Mattie and Pferden, to see someone he knew personally from the upcountry.

"Hey you, Oren," he said to one lean woodie, "you misters keep coming, you going to crowd out the farmers entirely. Thought you was the one said swamp otters are no use except for hides."

"Guess I was wrong, Cary," said Oren. "You was right; and no upcountry mister'll be raising gun or trap to otters from now on, like you always said we shouldn't. Guess too,

146.

if it was really Arcadians voting, none but otters'd be going to the polls here. But as for crowding farmers—we woods folks got a right."

"Whose wagon d'you think's hauling this statue?" growled Pferden.

"Never you mind, mister," said Oren. "It's for everybody on Arcadia, that statue—but it's ourn, first after the otters, remember you that. Because we aren't likely to forget it ourselves, we upcountry misters!"

The sun set, and still the train escorting the wagon increased in numbers. For five or six meters on either side of the road now, the grain was being trampled flat by upcountry boots—something that made Pferden mutter under his breath. Steadily, the oxen pulled the wagon forward at their unvarying pace that was scarcely more than a brisk walk for a man, but which the oxen could keep up for forty-eight hours without pause, given food and water as they went. The rise of the moon, now down to a fingernail clipping, gave little light—but shortly thereafter, they began to see a glow of light on the horizon ahead.

"Alpha Center," said Pferden. "We'll pass through there at midnight, easy—and from then on there'll be highway wide enough for these upcountry trampers to leave the fields alone."

"How far from there to the City?" asked Mattie. It was almost the first word she had said as she sat between Pferden and Cary on the wagon seat. Cary looked at her.

"Make the City by dawn easy, from Alpha Center," said Pferden. He chuckled. "Some of these woodies maybe'll find themselves under lock for the night if they don't behave themselves going through the Center, though. Our Beta Center's not bad, but Alpha's a real little city."

147.

He referred to this again when at last they did come out on the short stretch of wide-paved cement highway just before the city limits of Alpha Center.

"See there," he said, with a chuckle, pointing ahead. "Regular line of police hovercars set up across the road and out into the fields on each side. Word of this mob's gone ahead. They're going to see we walk nice and polite through their streets!"

He urged on the oxen and they pulled up until they were within a dozen meters of the line of police cars barring the road. There were police standing between and behind the cars, wearing light heat armor and carrying energy rifles.

"All right, that's far enough!" boomed a voice from the amplifier of the central hovercar.

Pferden cursed, startledly, sharply reining the oxen to a halt. Around and behind the wagon, the walkers stopped in chain reaction, like a caterpillar which has run its head up against an obstacle. The central car hissed up on its jets and slid forward, revealing another car in place behind it. It pulled up alongside the wagon, and a helmeted man looked out the window at Pferden, Cary, and Mattie up on the wagon seat.

"Turn around and get out of here—you and all the rest," the man under the helmet said. "The citizens of Alpha Center aren't letting any upcountry totem through their streets to break up the mortgage voting in Arcadia City tomorrow."

His gaze fastened on the tall form of Cary.

"You'll be Longan, I suppose," he said. "Well, listen to me. I've got two hundred armed and armored men there with police energy rifles. Take your fake statue and get this mob out of here or we'll open fire."

148.

13.

"Fifteen minutes?" said Cary calmly. "Sure, mister."

He turned to Pferden.

"Turn the wagon around, Svart," he said.

Pferden blinked at him without moving. Mattie stared, then exploded.

"Turn around! Just like that?" She turned on the helmeted man in the police hovercar. "Who do you think you are, telling us to turn around? The people in Alpha Center don't own the road through their town, or anything like it! The streets belong to all the citizens of Arcadia; and these are citizens on their way in to vote on the new mortgage—or not to vote, according to their consciences—"

"Mattie," said Cary.

She broke off, staring at him.

"Let's go," he said softly, and turned to Pferden once more. "I said, turn her around, Svart."

Pferden was also staring at him. But now, slowly, he picked up the reins and began to turn the wagon around. Mul and the woodsmen around the wagon were already passing back the word of what had been encountered up front.

By the time the wagon was turned around, the crowd of marchers behind it had parted to let it go back the way it had come; and many of the woodsmen were also turned around and ambling away from Alpha Center. A bright light shone suddenly around and beyond the wagon from behind it. The police hovercar had turned its spotlight on the wagon.

"Keep moving," said Cary to Pferden, who grunted angrily under his breath, but obeyed.

"But, Cary. . . ." Mattie began and then stopped at the sight of his face, which was now thin and tight. Ahead of them the crowd of woodies who had followed them were thinning out—they almost seemed to be evaporating into thin air—so that it could be seen that there had been a considerable percentage of farmers among them after all. Then, right in front of the plodding oxen, a woodie put a friendly arm on Jay Arrens and led the young man off into the dark, shoulder-high grain to the side of the road. The other farmers, like the woodies, began to disappear into the grain.

"*Five minutes left—then we open fire!*" boomed the amplified voice from the police car.

"Sound right eager, don't they?" commented Mul.

"I thought we passed a track going off just about back here, someplace," said Cary. "There it is. Turn the team down that, would you, Mister Pferden?"

Pferden hauled on the reins and the oxen turned off down the road onto a dirt wagon path going away through the grain.

"Now what?" said Pferden, once they were on this new track. There was a crackle of energy weapons, back at the police barricade.

150.

"Don't guess they hit anyone—everybody'd be out of sight by now," said Cary.

"Energy weapons can't hit what they can't see," commented Mul from alongside the wagon. "We'll just round up some of our upcountry misters with their long guns—"

"No," said Cary. "Maybe a couple of weeks ago, I'd have thought of that myself. But this is something different we got here in the wagon, what Charlie did. Using guns wouldn't just work out with it. What we got to do is vote, not shoot, if we want to keep Arcadia natural and sweet without a second mortgage. Mul, why don't you slide off around and pass the word for as many of our misters from upcountry with names everybody knows—them like Pid Gewaters, Haf Miron, and the like—big men. Tell them they can find me and the statue at a farmhouse around here someplace. You guess there'll be some farmhouse that'd put us up, Mister Pferden?"

"There'll be," said Pferden, economically.

"And maybe Mister Pferden will likewise ask around for those farmers that the other farmers all know about?" Cary looked at Pferden, who nodded. "Come morning we'll all get together at the farmhouse and talk this thing over."

"Right," said Mul, and disappeared into the grain.

Pferden drove on until the track ended in a farmyard. He went up to the door, which opened, and he talked to the silhouette of a woman seen against the light inside the house. He came back.

"Missus of the house, Miz Canameer," said Pferden, "says she'd be honored to have you come in. Mister Canameer should be home directly. He was out to join us when we were on the road."

They went in.

151.

Four hours later Mattie was still sleeping in the bedroom to which Miz Canameer had taken her. But Cary, who had also gotten some sleep, was up and facing some half-dozen men, half-farmers, half-woodies, in the farmhouse kitchen.

"Heard you didn't want guns used," said Haf Miron. He was a big, thick-necked woodie with a scar on his chin. "So we all passed the word to the misters. Don't see why, though. No hundred—two hundred—police going to trouble us."

"If it comes to that," said a heavy-bodied farmer, "we don't need no woodies to clear the police out of the way. Enough land people here to do that chore and never notice."

"How many farm people are there?" Cary asked the last speaker.

"Counting those that came in for Voting Day," said the man, "thirty thousand maybe, who could make it to City this morning."

Cary looked over at Haf Miron.

"And the upcountry people," he said. "How many?"

"Fifteen-twenty thousand," said Haf. "Misters been coming in all week."

"That's a lot of people," said Cary. "Enough to vote down the mortgage. You see why we don't want to use guns, no way. If we start shooting, we give those who want to mortgage again a chance to say we scared off their voters, and the voting don't count."

"That statue got to come in though," said Haf Miron. "If the statue stays out of the City, everybody'll figure the mortgage people got us licked."

"We'll get it in," said Cary.

"How?" asked the heavy-bodied farmer.

Cary laughed, his noiseless woodsman's laugh.

152.

"In two hours we'll hitch up Mister Pferden's team and move out," he said. "Just all of you go spread the word to tell the City folk that thirty thousand farmers and fifteen thousand upcountry people are coming in to see Charlie's statue brought to town."

Two hours later Pferden's wagon rumbled back out of the farmyard and onto the wagon track. Mattie, still sleepy-eyed, stared around them in astonishment.

"Where did all the people come from?" she said.

For the track was lined with farmers and woods people alike. As the wagon passed, they fell in behind it. Their numbers grew; and by the time the wagon pulled once more up on the road, it was surrounded by faces for fifteen meters in every direction.

They started once more down the road toward the City. Ahead, as on the wagon track, people stood waiting on either side along the way, peering at the statue as the wagon passed. But when the oxen approached the place where the police barricade had been the night before, there was nothing but open road. They continued on toward the City.

"Cary," said Mattie, "we've done it."

"Not yet, maybe," he said.

She looked at him oddly. But when they approached the edge of the City proper, her face tightened. Standing across the road before them was a line of police double the size they had faced the night before, this time armed with light energy cannon and holding back the sea of farmers and woods people that stood waiting.

"Keep going," said Cary to Pferden.

They drove on until the nose of the left ox was almost touching the jacket of the Captain of Police, who stood in the center of the roadway. The Captain was a narrow-faced man, perhaps a shade paler than normal, but determined.

"We're not letting you by, Longan," he said.

Cary, sitting on the front seat of the wagon, beside Pferden, nodded. He sat silent. The Police Captain waited, and time stretched out.

"Well?" demanded the Captain. "What are you going to do?"

"Nothing," said Cary.

"Nothing?" the Captain stared at him.

"That's right," said Cary. "You're not going to let us pass, so I guess we just have to sit here."

He went back to silence. The Captain stared at him a moment longer, then turned and walked up and down the length of the line of his men, checking weapons. He came back after a while to where the wagon sat. The oxen were patiently standing. Behind the oxen were Pferden, Cary, and Mattie; and behind and surrounding these, the multitude of farmers and woods people, also silently waiting. The Captain looked out over the ocean of standing people, then back at Cary.

"You're still not getting through," he said to Cary.

"Look behind you," said Cary.

The Captain turned, and stiffened. From out of the City behind his double line of armed men, a second crowd of people were forming—City people obviously, but waiting as quietly as the farmers and upcountry people without.

"Count off!" shouted the Police Captain. "By twos!"

"One . . . Two . . . One . . . Two . . ." The count went along the double line as each policeman counted up or down from the man next to him.

"Odd numbers," ordered the Captain. "About-face!"

Every other policeman in the line wheeled about with his weapon. Now half of them faced outward toward the country people and half faced inward toward their own City dwellers.

"Mul," said Cary, in the silence following this maneuver, "would you and some of the boys come help me? Long as we can't take Charlie's statue into the City, maybe we can stand it up here, so the folks can see it."

"Coming," said Mul.

He and everyone else standing nearby was scrambling into the wagon. Tanned hands took hold of the dark stone and heaved, then heaved again. The statue Charlie had carved rose upright in the wagon, tottered a moment, and stood still. Those who had lifted it dropped away over the wagon's sides.

The eyes of those on both sides of the police line went to the statue; and a slow, deep sound, like the sound of wind over a sea, swept across them as each one of them reacted to the sight. There was a surge on both sides of the line of police toward the armed men.

"No!" shouted Cary, standing up on the wagon seat. "No violence. That's not what Charlie carved it for!"

The surge sagged back. Once more the crowd stood still. The line of police stood still. The sun was warming, rising high in the sky.

"What are you trying to do?" whispered the Captain up at Cary.

"I'm waiting—only waiting," Cary answered, sitting down on the wagon seat once more.

The minutes crawled slowly by. Suddenly, down the line of police, there was movement. One of the men there had dropped his energy rifle and broken ranks. He was walking toward the wagon.

"Briggens!" shouted the Captain. "Get back in rank!"

Briggens paid no attention. He moved forward into a crowd of bodies that parted before him and closed after him, shielding him from the handgun the Captain had just drawn. He came forward at last to the very edge of the wagon and stood looking up at the statue. Then, slowly and deliberately, he took off his uniform cap and stripped away the pistol belt he wore.

Once more, sound rumbled through the crowd—but this time it was the word being passed back of what had happened by the wagon; and this time the sound maintained and mounted in volume toward a roar of triumph. Other policemen were breaking ranks, throwing down their weapons and mingling with the crowds on both sides.

"Mister Pferden," said Cary. "Time to move, I guess."

Pferden whistled at his oxen and picked up his reins. The two big beasts began to move forward, and the police melted away before them.

"No!" shouted the Captain. "No, you—"

He aimed his handgun at the wagon, and a moment later the crowd swallowed him up before he could fire. The steady legs of the oxen moved on toward the City. Men had already sprung from the crowd about, into the wagon to hold the statue upright; and upright it entered into the City.

The sun was above the buildings at full noon when the wagon rumbled finally through the streets of Arcadia City to stop across the street from the same hotel in which Lige Bros Waters had greeted Cary, two weeks before. People—city people, farmers, and woodies, particularly the last—filled the street about it and spilled over to choke the park facing the hotel where the voting booths had been set up. As the wagon reached the park, Cary put his hand on Pferden's shoulder.

156.

"Stop here," he said. "Don't let them unload the statue yet."

"Cary!" cried Mattie, as Cary swung himself down from the seat of the wagon. "You're not going for that buyer *now,* are you? You aren't going to try to sell Charlie's statue with what it means now to all these people? What'll stop the mortgage being voted in then?"

Cary's face was grim.

"Asked Mister Waters come back to see. My word, my deal," he said. He turned swiftly and went across the street into the hotel, not looking back. In the lobby he hunted down the list of those in residence, found Waters's name, and pressed the call button.

"Who?" asked a computerized voice.

"Cary Longan," Cary said. "To see Mister Lige Bros Waters."

There was a second's pause.

"Admitted," said the voice. Beside the list, one of the elevator doors slid open. Cary stepped in, rode up, and stepped out to search down a corridor of doors for the one bearing the name Waters. He spoke to the door.

"I know that voice," said the black annunciator circle on the door. "Come in." Cary touched the door, and it opened before him. Inside was the art buyer, looking no different than the last time Cary had seen him.

"That statue," Cary said, as he stepped into the room. "I brought it. But things are some different—"

"So I gather." Lige Waters's voice was old and hard and dry. He waved to the window on the far wall showing a view of the street before the hotel and the park beyond it. "What's it doing out there?"

"Out there?" Cary stepped closer to the screen.

157.

The statue was no longer in the wagon. It had been removed, and taken into a central part of the park among the trees facing the voting booths. It stood upright there, leaning a little to one side, evidently because the cut across the stone of its base had not been level. But to all intents and purposes the carved stone stood vertical enough. A line of people flowed into the park, moving slowly past it, each one pausing a little to examine it before pressure from the line behind forced him to move on. They were woodsmen mostly in the line; but there were farmers as well, and astonishingly, not a few men and women in city clothes, patiently waiting their turn with the rest.

"Let's go down," said Lige. "I want to look at it up close."

They went down, across the street, and into the park. To one side behind the statue and its passing line, stood a little knot of people—Mattie, Mul, Pferden, Haf Miron, and a farmer Cary did not recognize.

"Mattie," Cary said as he and Lige came up, "what's this?"

She swung about to him, stiff-backed.

"I'll tell you what it is!" she said. "You can't sell it without my permission—and I'm not giving it." She glanced at Lige. "Do you hear that, looper? This statue's not for sale."

Lige's face drew in until it was wrinkled and grim, like the face of an old snapping turtle from Earth.

"I've been hearing how you got into this business, Miss—"

"Orvalo."

"—Miss Orvalo," said Lige. "I should tell you. I've got the recording of a verbal contract with this man, that antedates any deal you may have made with him. You can sue him if you want to, but you can't stop any sale to me."

"See you dead first, mister," said Haf Miron, casually from the side. Lige turned his snapping-turtle face, unmoved, to look at the big, scarred woodsman.

"Interworld business is a little bigger than you think, friend," he said. "The company I work for can get a pan-stellar judgment giving them the statue, and if your local courts won't execute it, we'll embargo all your off-world trade. Even, if necessary, get a Union Navy ship in here to make collection."

"We don't care—" Mattie was beginning.

"Hush, Mattie. You too, Haf," said Cary. "My word, my deal. I'll do the talking." He turned to Lige. "Like I started to say back upstairs, mister, things are some different from when I first talked to you about Charlie's statue. Guess maybe we could sell you something other instead. Maybe those little statues of Charlie's I showed you first."

Lige's head turned sharply to him.

"Told you I didn't see anything worth buying in those lumps!" he said. "What makes you think I'd change my mind now?"

Cary gazed quietly at him.

"Back then you didn't sound like you had much interest in talking a deal," Cary said. "Now you do. Guess if you see something worth buying in the statue there now, you'd see its like in the little statues, once you look them over again."

Lige stared back at him, then slowly moved his gaze to the statue.

"All right," Lige said. "Maybe there's something here. Not much—but something. Maybe I'd have seen it for myself, even if I hadn't heard and seen how all your people here are being moved by it. Or maybe I needed to see them looking to go looking myself. I've been in business long

159.

enough to know that there's no single person knows all there is to know about art. But that doesn't have to say I was wrong when I didn't see anything the first time I looked at those things you call little statues."

"Doesn't have to say it," said Cary. "But you know now you were, don't you, mister?"

The snapping-turtle face jerked back to Cary. It was a moment before the art dealer spoke.

"And even if I did see something in the small statues now, after all," he went on, "a boxful of small pieces aren't going to make up for losing a life-size work that's got a whole world of people acting as if they just discovered religion. I'd need a lot more small pieces to make up for that —and the word I hear is your native—that swamp otter, or whatever—who carved this is dead."

Cary nodded.

"Charlie's dead," he said. "But all his people carve some. Their teeth keep growing all their lives, so they've got to keep them worn down. So they all work on stones—some better, some worse. I can get you as many of those you want."

Lige glared at him.

"Listen," he said, "do you know—have you any idea how many men there've been with no art in them at all, compared to one great artist?"

"Point isn't how many weren't artists. Point is, more'n one was," said Cary. "That's right, isn't it?"

He pointed to the statue. Lige still glared at him, saying nothing.

"Mister," said Cary, "you better deal with me—because there's no one else for you to deal with. You want to buy those small statues of Charlie's instead of this big one, and for me to go back to the upcountry and get you more of what his people did? Or not?"

The grim and wrinkled face slowly relaxed. Slit-mouthed, he nodded.

"But these carvings by the other swamp otters," he said, "better be worth it!"

"They are," said Cary. "But you could use them even if they weren't, couldn't you, mister?"

Lige's old face went suddenly pale, then flooded with dark surging color.

"Come on! *Cary.*" Mattie pulled hastily at Cary's elbow before the art dealer could speak. "You come on with me, right now! You need to shave and clean up. We've got to draw up new articles of partnership, and besides there's things I want to talk to you about. . . ."

Talking unceasingly, she drew Cary away. After a first second of hesitation, he smiled, and let himself be drawn. Lige stared at their retreating backs, at first wordlessly, then finding his voice to yell after them.

"I buy *art,* you young backwoods hick!" Lige shouted. "ART. . . ."

Neither Cary nor Mattie turned their heads, nor slowed their pace. The color fading slowly from his face, Lige turned back to the statue and saw Haf, with the others, watching him.

"And the rest of you," he snarled, "don't fool yourselves. Maybe there's art in that thing there"—he jabbed a finger at the statue—"but it's about the level of a child playing with clay. It's the art of a stone-age savage painting buffalo on the wall of a cave. A spoonful of art to a whole wagon-sized chunk of stone. It's got some accidental form to it and a little lucky deliberate shaping that lets your eye read something into it that may or may not be there at all. Real art's not like that—accidental. Real art's unmistakable—it reaches out and takes hold of you and makes you into something different. I know! And if there was art like *that,* there in that thing, I'd see it."

Haf looked back at the dealer, then swung his woodsman's gaze over to the voting booths, now no longer with lines of people waiting to sign up for the second mortgage. It was not yet noon, and already the booths were standing empty. A second mortgage would have required enough signatures to keep the booths busy all day. Haf looked away from the booths, back to the endless line of people filing past the statue.

"Mister," he said to Lige, "you're blind."

About Gordon R. Dickson

by

Sandra Miesel

In Gordon R. Dickson's action-filled universe, grim fighting men and Buddha-faced mystics jostle teddy bears in spacesuits; dolphins leap and dragons prowl; indomitable heroes reshape heaven and earth by force of will or take bumpy rides in mailbags, construct analog models of the cosmos or befriend the Loch Ness Monster.

After nearly 40 novels and 175 shorter works spread over three decades, this motley band of character-types has brought Dickson from a subsistence diet of stale bread and peanut butter to the acclaim of his public and the esteem of his peers. He won the Hugo Award for "Soldier, Ask Not" (1965) and the Nebula Award for "Call Him Lord" (1966). From 1969 to 1971 he served as President of the Science Fiction Writers' Association and is a legendary mainstay of sf fan gatherings.

Dickson wanted to be a writer from his earliest years. He entered the University of Minnesota in 1939 at age 15 to study creative writing. After time out for military service during World War II, he completed his Bachelor of Arts degree in 1948. He withdrew from graduate school to become a full-time writer in 1950 and has been at it ever since. He is one of the few sf authors to have made writing his sole occupation.

Both training and natural inclination have made Dickson unusually attentive to matters of literary craftsmanship, not only in his own work, but in the sf field as a whole. He works tirelessly to upgrade performance standards through lectures, convention appearances, and even private conversations. His dedication to deliberate craft and philosophical argument combines what he calls the "consciously thematic novel"—the adventure story with a moral. As the author himself explains: "The action of the thematic novel is in no way loaded . . . with a bias towards proving the author's point. . . . The aim is to make the theme such an integral part of the novel that it can be effective on the reader without ever having to be stated explicitly."

Dickson has a compelling interest in the theory as well as the practice of artistic creativity. He studies—and writes about—issues like creative overdrive, performance under stress, interactions between different skills, and the social impact of gifted individuals. This stems from his conviction that man's proper destiny is to grow ever more creative. He sees unlimited potential for achievement in man and all other intelligent beings.

The highest and clearest expression of Dickson's views is found in his Childe Cycle. When complete, the Cycle will dramatize humanity's coming of age from the fourteenth century to the twenty-fourth in a series of twelve novels—three historical, three contemporary, and three science fictional. *Dorsai!* (1959), *Necromancer* (1962), "Warrior" (1965), *Soldier, Ask Not* (1968), *Tactics of Mistake* (1971), and "Brothers" (1973) have appeared so far. The last pair of sf novels, *The Final Encyclopedia* and *Childe*, are currently in preparation. The author expects to spend the rest of his working life completing and polishing the Cycle.

The Cycle is a grand synthesis of Dickson's favorite themes

and motifs. (However, a few germs of these can even be found in early novels like *Time to Teleport*, 1955 and *Mankind on the Run*, 1956.) The Cycle treats the human race like a single organism in which the condition of each individual cell affects the health of the whole. The progressive and conservative tendencies of this human organism, symbolized as estranged Twin Brothers, must be reconciled if the organism is to continue growing. Specialized, sometimes tightly organized, groups work to ease the problem but it can only be solved by the combined efforts of the Three Prime Characters—the Men of Faith, Philosophy, and War. When fully mature, humanity will exercise creative and responsible control over its own evolution.

But although the Cycle is Dickson's masterpiece, not all his fiction is that serious. (In fact, *Delusion World*, 1961 parodies the Cycle.) One showcase for his broad, bouncy sense of humor is the popular Hoka series written in collaboration with his close friend Poul Anderson. (Comedy is the only area in which these two dissimilar authors' attitudes and writing styles coincide.) As related in *Earthman's Burden* (1955) and *Star Prince Charlie* (1975), the Hokas are cuddly, bright-eyed aliens resembling teddy bears who have a mad flair for mimicry. They love to play at being cowboys or Foreign Legionnaires or other human adventure heroes to the endless frustration of the human diplomat stationed on their planet. These stories, like most of Dickson's humorous work, are based on the plight of a rational being in a preposterously irrational situation.

Whether he is writing seriously or humorously, Dickson makes thrifty use of his own experiences and interests as fictional raw material. Because he was born in Canada and has spent most of his adult life in Minneapolis, he often uses Canadian and Midwestern settings to good effect. The quest for authenticity works both ways. For instance, it has led him to order a complete suit of fourteenth century armor as a research tool for writing medieval novels. Likewise, Dickson's fondness for literature, history, art, music, martial arts, and physical fitness is clearly evident in his work. Since he himself quotes Kipling, sings, composes songs, paints, and works out, so do many of his characters. Needless to say, artistically gifted action heroes are a novelty in sf.

The wolves, dolphins, whales, great cats, and other beasts populating Dickson's stories reflect his fascination with animals and animal behavior. (Appropriately, his heraldic badge in the Society for Creative Anachronism is an otter.) This carries over into his treatment of intelligent extraterrestrials. Beings like the Atakit in *Alien from Arcturus* (1956) are directly modeled on familiar animals.

In conclusion, Dickson's work is the product of a keen, inquisitive mind purposefully shaping ideas into art. His stories are deliberately constructed, not casually improvised. He weaves structural and symbolic patterns into his fictional fabric to express philosophical convictions. At its serious best, his style is efficient, austere, almost relentless, like swift-running streams of icy water or beams of wintry northern light. C. S. Lewis's description of Norse myth applies equally well to Dickson's writing: "cold, spacious, severe, pale, and remote."

ISAAC ASIMOV